Suddenly . . .

more men swarmed around either side of the sheer rock face, all dressed in white, like German ski soldiers of World War II. Each had a small silver dove embroidered on the material over his heart.

Blenkochev raised a hand full of command.

"I am Blenkochev," he said majestically in his cultured Russian. "I've caught the notorious Nick Carter. He's the imperialist AXE agent from that overweight pig, the United States."

NICK CARTER IS IT!

FROM THE NICK CARTER KILLMASTER SERIES

NICK CARTER

KILLMASTER

White Death

CHARTER BOOKS, NEW YORK

WHITE DEATH

A Charter Book/published by arrangement with
The Condé Nast Publications, Inc.

PRINTING HISTORY
Charter edition/August 1985

ISBN: 0-441-88568-3

Charter Books are published by The Berkley Publishing Group,
200 Madison Avenue, New York, New York 10016.
PRINTED IN THE UNITED STATES OF AMERICA

ONE

The blood spread thick and scarlet over the fisherman's vest. It was a tidy pool of blood, slowly sloughing down the dead man's chest. He was resting comfortably back against a pine tree, his fishing rod in his hand, waiting for a bite.

The remote mountain stream rushed and sang among ferns and moss-covered boulders. The New Zealand air was crisp and clear, sparkling with the throbbing calls of birds. Nick Carter moved forward silently and set his tackle box and rod on the sloping bank. He squatted in front of the dead man.

The instrument of death was a highly sophisticated poison dart fired from a rifle at great distance. It was a weapon used most often by international agents. The killing had been expertly quiet, performed sometime in the last fifteen minutes. The blood was fresh, warm. The killer had known where to find his target. By now, he would have disappeared.

Carter felt the dead man's pockets and took out the wallet. Jerome Mackenzie, the driver's license said, forty-two years old, height five-eleven, weight one-eighty, address in Wellington. What the license didn't say was that the man was also head of New Zealand's civil air authority.

Carter checked the other pockets, and found cash, coins, a pocketknife, and a toothpick in a silver case. He went through the sack lunch and the tackle box filled with flies and weights. Nothing of any use.

He sat back, rubbing the new beard on his chin. He was on vacation. Some vacation. He picked up his gear and walked back to the road.

The mountain police station was built of timbers, with a long porch that abutted other rough buildings in the small village. Tall trees swayed overhead while villagers shopped and rode jeeps up and down the single paved road. Dogs barked. A sheep in a pen behind the gas station chewed thoughtfully on hay.

Inside the police headquarters, Nick Carter nursed a cup of lukewarm coffee and smiled into the suspicious eyes of the local police chief.

"You're telling me that you came all the way from the United States just to talk to Mackenzie?" the chief said.

He had a broad face the color of old leather. Sun and wind had weathered his skin and thinned his patience. He drummed his fingers on the arm of his chair.

"Vacation," Carter said again. "A friend in Washington asked me to look Mackenzie up since I was already here. See whether Mackenzie knew anything about a missing American flyer named Rocky Diamond."

"Rocky Diamond? You expect me to believe a name like that?"

Carter shrugged. The irony of the situation made him smile. He'd used the ruse of being on vacation many times in his work. He was N3, Killmaster with AXE, the most secret of all United States espionage agencies. The ruse usually worked. But now that he really had time off, this small-town policeman in the hinterlands of New Zealand who had no idea who Carter really was had no intention of believing him.

"That's the name," Carter said. "Check it with Wellington."

He stroked his cheeks, feeling the new beard soft against his fingers. Dammit. He wanted this vacation!

"It's being checked," the police chief growled. "Tourists, deer rustlers, marijuana plantations! I might as well be in Auckland!'' He stood and marched to the window. ''Laws to wear seat belts and license your dog. Parrots that eat the weatherstripping off your car's windshield.'' Annoyance at acts of government and God flushed the chief's face as if they were directed solely at him. He turned to Carter.

''I only found him,'' Carter said mildly.

''But *how* did you know where to find him? Were *you* planning to kill him too?''

''My friend in Washington,'' Carter explained. ''He was in touch with air authority officials in Wellington.''

''And this friend of yours?''

''Sorry. A high government official. Top secret. Can't give you a name.''

The police chief grimaced. He hadn't liked it the first time Carter had told him. He liked it less now.

''Seems there are a lot of things you can't tell me,'' the chief said. He poured hot coffee into his mug and sat again behind his desk. ''You say you're a chemical engineer from California on vacation, but that doesn't explain why some big shot in Washington wants you to do a secret job for him. You don't know why this Rocky Diamond is important. You don't know anything about Jerome Mackenzie's murder. What *do* you know?''

Carter laughed.

''My coffee's cold,'' he said, and he reached for the pot on the edge of the chief's desk and poured. ''Look,'' he said and leaned back, ''I'd like to help, but I've only got a week's vacation. All I want is to fish and work on my beard. As it is, I've lost most of today. That leaves me only four more days, and the trout are biting. You've got my statement. My papers are in order. Why don't you do us both a favor and let me get out of here?''

The chief narrowed his eyes. His face was flushed. He had a murder in his precinct, and not of an ordinary local man. Mackenzie was out-of-district and important. Wellington, the nation's seat of government, would be on the chief's back. But he had no legal reason to hold Carter. He sighed.

"No reason to keep you, I suppose," he admitted. "But stay in the area."

"Glad to." Carter stood and drained his coffee cup. "Plenty of streams around here to keep me occupied."

As he picked up his hat, tackle box, and rod, the front door opened. He walked to the door.

A young patrolman, his face pocked with a lost battle against acne, strode in, a folded piece of paper in his hand.

"See you around," Carter told the chief, then started to leave.

"Noel Cash?" the patrolman said to Carter.

"That's right," Carter said, walking out onto the porch.

"Just a minute, sir," the patrolman said politely. He waited until Carter stopped.

Irritation prickled on the back of Carter's neck.

The patrolman handed the paper to the chief, and the chief read it. He looked up, and for the first time he smiled at Carter.

"Guess I'll have to lock you up," he said with pleasure. He stood, dropping the paper onto his desk. He pulled out a ring of keys. "Telegram says someone from Wellington will be here in an hour to question you."

Carter looked the two men up and down. The chief was heavyset, muscular. The young patrolman soon would be. The eager youth drew the pistol from his belt, pointed it at Carter, and motioned him to the timbered door at the back of the office.

Keeping order in their mountainous region had made them tough and strong. Probably canny, too. But Carter knew that with a few quick karate chops the chief and his junior would be immobile on the floor and Carter would be free.

It was the Killmaster's turn to sigh. He was on vacation. Nothing he could do.

"I'll go quietly," he said, mocking himself.

The chief nodded solemnly, missing the joke, and led Carter into a back hall lined with four cells.

The single occupant, housed in the first cell, snored loudly. The faint aroma of whiskey drifted from his cot.

"Harry won't bother you," the chief said cheerfully and nodded at the sleeping drunk. Now that he could turn Carter over to someone with greater authority, he could be agreeable. "Good-natured sort," he added and unlocked the end cell on the right. "In you go."

Carter walked through and turned. The cell door closed with a clang. The drunk snorted and rolled over. The chief turned the key, locking Carter in. The two police officers walked back into their office, talking, and closed the door.

Carter stood in the center of his small enclosure, surrounded by his long bars and the bars of the other cells. He was trapped in a forest of bars. There were trout streams out there waiting to be fished, and he was locked up. Fat rainbow and brown trout. For a moment he wished he were on assignment. Then at least he could break out of this damned cell.

He threw his gear under the cot and fell on the narrow bed. There was one small window, high up, barred. The afternoon sunlight shone through, making a bright rectangle on the floor sliced with the shadows of more bars.

He folded his hands behind his head and stared at the timbered ceiling. This was what he deserved for doing Hawk a favor. Just a couple of questions, Hawk had said. Nothing big. Shouldn't take much time at all.

He should never have answered the summons of the heat-radiant signal under his skin. He should never have made the telephone call to Hawk's office.

He closed his eyes, thoroughly disgusted. Outside, machinery hummed. People talked, laughed. Children shouted in play. The smell of pines in the fresh mountain air beckoned. The time passed slowly.

He'd chosen New Zealand because it was a quiet nation in international politics. Not like countries in the Middle East, Southeast Asia, or Central America. It was two small islands, shaped like a comma at the bottom of the world: North Island, where he was now, and South Island. Its closest big neighbor nation was Australia, and Antarctica if one considered that frozen multinational continent a country.

The sheep behind the gas station bleated. Dogs barked and birds sang. Jeeps and trucks passed on the road. They were ordinary sounds in a country known for its peacefulness and lack of international intrigue. And this was where Nick Carter, the premier Killmaster, one of the best agents in the world, was jailed.

At last the door from the office opened. The chief sauntered in, followed by a tall woman with flowing chestnut hair. The drunk still snored, lost in his world of dreams.

"There he is," the chief announced, his lined face wrinkling even more in an enormous smile. Relief had vastly improved his disposition. He gestured grandiosely at Carter and unlocked the cell door. "He's all yours."

"Thanks," the woman said. She had vibrant blue eyes and a long shapely body encased in a tight jump suit glued to her curves. She paced into the cell. "I'll interrogate him alone," she told the chief, her gaze fixed on Carter. A small smile played at the corners of her mouth. "Top secret," she explained.

The chief shrugged. "Whatever you say," he said, then locked the door as he left.

She was Michelle Strange, known in international agent circles as Mike, a top agent of New Zealand intelligence, closely allied with MI6 in London. Since New Zealand had so few agents, they could afford to be picky. With her, they'd gotten both brains and beauty.

Carter watched her from his cot, and grinned.

She threw her shoulder bag to the floor and glared at him.

"You bastard!" she snarled. "How come you're in New Zealand without calling me?"

TWO

Michelle Strange vibrated with energy. The flowing chestnut hair that curled at her shoulders bounced angrily. Her hands worked the air as she talked.

"How dare you!" she stormed. "We've been together too many times. You insensitive lout! Where are your manners? If I know you're around, I always call *you*. Vacation. Ha!"

"Mike . . . "

Nick Carter rolled off the cot.

"Don't you Mike me!" She stamped her foot.

"Now, Mike," he said with a smile. "I was going to call you. Really."

He reached to stroke her cheek. She slapped his hand away.

"As soon as I got back from fishing," he said and grinned.

"Even when I'm on a job, I call you!"

"You don't want a smelly fisherman," he said. "You want an exciting agent."

She turned her back.

"Who says I want you at all?"

He slid a hand up under the mane of hair and kissed the back of her neck.

"A beard, too," she said. "Yeechh."

Her skin tasted fresh, of perfumed bathwater. He ran his hands down her back, over the rounded hips, up her sides. She squirmed but didn't move away.

7

"I'm not this easy," she said.

"You're never easy," he said. "Just beautiful. Desirable."

She leaned back.

Carter trailed his fingers around the outlines of her full breasts, then cupped them in his hands. She sighed deep in her throat. He rubbed his thumbs on the nipples. She ground her hips into him. Her head turned, taking in the four cells.

"We're not alone," she said, watching the sleeping drunk who continued to snore peacefully.

Carter turned her around. Her head fell back, the lips parted.

"Do you care?" he asked.

She pulled his head down.

They kissed, her lips hot and moist. He unzipped her jump suit, then leaned away to look at her. The breasts fell out, pink and ripe.

"The chief could come any minute," she breathed.

He smiled, then pulled the shoulders of the jump suit down to her feet.

She was stark naked. Not a wisp of underwear. All curves and lines. Pink skin showed a reverse silhouette of a bikini, the rest tanned to honey by the New Zealand summer sun. The breasts swayed. The triangle of chestnut hair where her legs met were soft springy curls.

He slid his hand between the legs. She unzipped his pants and moaned. He felt the hot slipperiness of her.

She grabbed him around the waist and pulled him between her legs, arching her back. Blood pounded into his head. She bit his ear.

Gently they began moving together, her hips grinding against him. Her movements became shorter, frenzied, fighting herself.

Until she exploded. Screamed into his shoulder. A muffled animal sound of defeat and triumph.

He picked her up, swollen with desire, and carried her to the cot. She raked her nails over his back, whimpering.

More. She wanted more.

He lay her on the edge, her feet dangling to the floor, and knelt between her legs. She lifted her head, looking at him with startled blue eyes. Eyes glazed into new need.

He pulled her legs up over his shoulders and thrust into her. Hard man, soft woman. She reared up, exploding again. Face twisted. Lips and teeth biting off a scream.

Thunder rolled through him. Rocked him into her until he too exploded in the black heat of victory.

Petit mort, the little death that man and woman achieve at orgasm. The thought made Carter smile. He lay sweating next to Mike. The little death that brought new life, new vigor. He should have called her.

She stroked his beard.

"It's very short," she observed, studying his jaw.

He chuckled.

"Right now I'm short all over."

She ran her hand down his belly. "Awww . . . " Damn that woman.

"I think you ought to shave it," she said.

"What??"

She laughed quietly.

"The beard, you dope." She lay back, smiling contentedly. "We've got to leave soon. The chief was eager to pass you on to me, but his curiosity will get the best of him eventually."

"You're breaking me out?"

"I've got the authority. The chief will send you off with hugs and kisses."

"He's not my type."

She laughed again. He looked at his fishing gear.

"You like to fish?" he said.

"Stop it, Nick," she said and grinned. "We have to talk business. Then I'll see about getting you out. Now, what's all this about Mackenzie?"

"I don't know any more than what I told the chief."

She looked at him with narrowed eyes. She was changing back to the old Mike. Stiff. Professional. Distrusting. She rolled over him and stood, a suspicious virago with a halo of wild chestnut hair. More beautiful than ever.

He had to smile.

"Cut the crap, Nick," she snapped. "What the hell's going on?" She picked up her clothes.

"Far as I can tell, it's a civil air authority matter."

"Don't give me any of that CAA garbage. AXE doesn't work on CAA matters."

"Never has before."

"You're lying to me. I know it. What does AXE want in New Zealand?"

She stepped into her jump suit, wriggled it up around her hips, and tucked in the flushed breasts.

"I'm the only AXE operative here," he said, still smiling. "All I want's my vacation. Can you get some time off too?"

She glared at him. The blue eyes flashed. She zipped up the jump suit.

"Mackenzie was killed by an expert, and for some damned big reason," she said. "We don't have sophisticated killers like that in New Zealand."

"Investigating that sounds more like your job than mine."

"Not if AXE killed him."

"That means you think I killed him."

He gathered his clothes, threw them on the cot, and began to dress. The drunk writhed on his cot and snorted.

"Wha'zit?" Harry the drunk said, batting the air. He sat up abruptly, punching imaginary demons. "Goddamnit all! Bloody thieves!" He opened his eyes and looked around.

Carter buttoned his shirt.

"What about Mackenzie himself?" Carter asked Mike quietly. "Maybe he knew something he shouldn't."

"I miss anything?" the drunk asked, watching Carter and Mike with bleary eyes. "Sorry if I disturbed you," he slurred.

Carter laughed.

"You didn't bother us a bit. Have a good nap?"

Harry rubbed his eyes and swung his legs over the edge of the cot.

"Ohhhh," he groaned, sinking back.

"You bastard," Mike hissed at Carter. "I want to know what's going on! What did you want Mackenzie for?"

"Like I told the chief," Carter said. "I was asked to do a favor, to find out from the man whether he had any information about a missing American flyer. A real maverick. Rocky Diamond."

She stared hard at him and finally nodded.

"Chief Merritt!" she shouted at the office door. "I'm finished!"

She picked up her shoulder bag, and Carter gathered his fishing gear. The sky showed gray with silvery clouds through the small cell window. It was dusk. Mountain night would fall quickly. Carter would get some sleep and be out at daybreak to fish. He could already smell the moist morning air, hear the jump-splash of the trout.

The chief strode down the hallway toward them, keys in hand.

"Hey, Marshal," the drunk called, sitting up again. "Time to let me out?"

"Not yet, Harry," the chief said and smiled. "Get a good meal. Spend the night."

The drunk nodded thoughtfully from his cot.

"You ready?" Chief Merritt asked Mike.

"Right."

The chief unlocked the cell, and she walked through, Carter following. She grabbed the barred door and slammed it shut in his face.

"Mike!"

"He's lying through his teeth," she told the chief. "Hold him for the inquest, and watch him closely!"

She stalked down the hall. The drunk stood up and stumbled to the wall of bars. He grabbed two bars, steadied himself, and watched her.

"Bloody good-looking broad," he observed.

"Dammit, Mike!" Carter shouted.

The chief glanced at Carter, his weatherbeaten face amused. Then he remembered that he still had Carter, alias Noel Cash, on his hands. He frowned, locked the cell, and stuffed the keys in his pocket.

"Wait!" he called to Mike. "I'll get the door for you!"

He ran ahead to open the office door for Mike, an important government official from Wellington with the two best legs he'd ever seen.

She glanced over her shoulder so that Chief Marshal Merritt couldn't see. She grinned wickedly at Carter, stuck out her tongue, and disappeared into the office. She wouldn't be back. The chief closed the door behind them.

Carter dropped his gear and flopped back on the cot.

"She yours?" the drunk wanted to know. "I mean, if I'd had one like that . . ." He paused, remembering. "It's enough to make a man stop the drink," he decided.

The bomb exploded in a burst of light and heat.

The impact thundered through the jail. The outside wall of the cell between Carter and the drunk blasted open. Timbers, big pieces of wood, and splinters slashed through the air. The cots rattled and jumped. One toilet flushed spontaneously.

Part of the wall in Harry the drunk's cell disintegrated in the explosion. He held onto his bars and looked reflectively back at the gaping hole. It wasn't that he particularly wanted to be free. But when the opportunity was provided on a silver platter, no one should ignore it. He ran toward the hole on wobbly legs.

"Stop!" Carter yelled at him. "You don't know what's out there!"

Carter's cell walls and bars were intact. The darkening night spilled shadows through the gap at the side of the jail. Outside, pines wavered, charcoal and black. "Harry, stop!"

But Harry ran out. He never looked back over his shoulder. It was the principle of the thing.

Instantly the rifle shots rang out, punctuating the village's stunned silence. The first bullet entered the left lobe of Harry's lung and exited through his back. The second bullet caught him as he stumbled with surprise at the pain. It entered the top of his cranium and blew the back of his head off.

THREE

The second explosion occurred almost instantly. It shattered the wall of the cell across from Nick Carter. Carter dropped to the floor. Shouts and curses filled the air. Gunfire streaked through the night. It was the two policemen, villagers . . . and who else?

The office door burst open. Hair flying, Mike Strange hit the light switch and ran down the short hall in the gloom. The young policeman, his pocked face contorted with fear and worry, ran with her.

"It's about time," Carter said.

"What the hell's happening around here?" she demanded.

"Don't really know." He smiled. "I'm on vacation, remember?"

"Vacation! Ha!" Mike said, handing him a .45. "Get in there!" she ordered the policeman.

As she unlocked Carter's cell, the young man unlocked and slipped into Harry's cell. The drunk lay outside, bloody, spread out like a rag doll. The bright light of a full moon glowed on his corpse.

Bullets sang through the hole in the drunk's cell wall. Carter and Mike dropped to the floor. The policeman fell flat, his forehead grazed by a bullet. Determined, shaking, he aimed and fired into the night.

"I can't see anything!" the young man said, shooting again.

Bullets ricocheted in the enclosure and bounced off the bars.

"Watch for their fire!" Carter told him from the floor. "You'll see the streaks of light."

Carter and Mike crawled to the cell opposite the drunk's where the second wall had been blasted open.

"This thing work?" Carter asked, pulling the trigger. It kicked in his hand, the bullet going harmlessly into the ground. It was a good gun, but not as good as Wilhelmina, his 9mm Luger.

"It'd better," Mike said. "Watch for the whites of their eyes!"

"You've been seeing too much television," Carter chuckled, then he concentrated on one of the darting shadows that weaved among the pines.

He squeezed the trigger. The figure's arms flew up, and the body keeled over backward.

Gunfire spattered from the side of the building, aimed at the shadowy movements in the trees.

"Chief Merritt?" Carter asked.

Mike nodded and fired. The figure in the distance doubled over and limped off.

"The chief's around the corner with a deputized friend," she said.

"Looks like about a dozen out there," Carter mused, watching for a target.

"We're outnumbered. We got a few, though."

Quietly the two agents concentrated on their work as the hot stench of gunfire slowly filled the jailhouse. They waited for the movements or telltale streaks of gunfire that would give them targets. Bullets occasionally whistled over their heads. They shot in return, often missing as the attackers disappeared behind trees and deep into shadows. The pine branches sang in a growing breeze, the eerie sound whining between the cracks of gunfire. Each pause between bullets lengthened. Tension thickened the air.

"It's too quiet," Mike whispered at last. "They're planning something."

Suddenly a burst of gunfire came from the young policeman behind them.

"They're coming!" he yelled, firing again and again.

Mike bolted.

"Come on!" she shouted at Carter.

Carter started to rise but thought better of it and dropped flat again.

"You go!"

She ran through the jail and flattened herself down next to the policeman. Carefully choosing her shots, she fired. It didn't sound like a major attack.

Carter slid to the side of the hole, his body hidden behind the ragged remains of the cell wall. He counted the seconds. If it was going to happen, it would be soon.

His sharp eyes studied the wavering darkness. Nothing. They were a gutsy group, the attackers. And they'd come prepared in dark clothing that blended with the night. They had accurate weapons, and there was something—or someone—in the jail that they wanted. Dead. They weren't fools. Carter couldn't believe that they would be so stupid as to . . .

Then he saw them. Four, spread out. Creeping toward what they hoped was an abandoned entrance. Then, with no bullets coming at them, they ran, confident, a coalescing juggernaut. The group on the other side of the jail that Mike and the young policeman fired at were a diversion. This small group before Carter was the one that expected to conquer the jail.

With the remarkably rapid reflexes that the Killmaster was legendary for—and that he hoped would keep him from getting killed—he leaned out beyond the ragged edge of the wall.

He aimed at the figure coming from his blind spot, and fired.

The body flew back into nothingness.

Carter ducked back.

Three bullets bit into the wall around Carter's head. Splinters flew. He jumped up and came out from a new spot. Bullets pummeled the spot where he'd been.

Quickly he aimed and fired twice.

Two more fell, as dark as coal against the black ground shadows.

A bullet sang into the wall, then another. Wood dust stung his eyes and he closed them, waiting for the soothing tears.

"What's going on?" Mike shouted from behind.

Carter knelt. He heard the feet pounding, light, but a heavy body that couldn't disguise its mass.

"Stay where you are!" Carter called back to Mike.

"They're hidden!" Mike said. "We can't get any of them. It's like shooting at ghosts!"

The attacker lunged through the door.

Carter's eyes flew open, his vision blurry. His eyes burned like fire.

The gun was a wavering black stick in the attacker's hand.

Carter rolled into the legs.

The gun came down, slicing the air.

Carter leaped up.

Aimed for the belly, kicked.

Missed, smashed the gun across the cell.

"Get out of the way, Nick!" Mike yelled, worried. "I can't get a clear shot!"

The big hands slashed toward Carter's neck. He saw the hands clearly. Thick hands with broad fingers accustomed to heavy work.

Carter reared back and smashed his elbow into the attacker's chest.

Ribs cracked. The attacker grunted and stepped aside.

Carter pulled back a fist that had power enough to flatten a gorilla. This man he'd take alive, then question.

The shot rang out.

"No!" Mike shouted. "Nick had him!"

The attacker's belly erupted. A volcano of blood spewed out. The blackened face of the attacker looked down at himself, stunned. Suddenly the jail and surroundings were quiet. He seemed to listen to the silence, then he pitched forward onto his knees, wobbled, and lifted a foot to stand. Helplessly Carter watched. The man was already dead. At last he acknowledged his end. He sank onto the floor in a sea of blood.

"Dammit, Perry," Mike complained sadly to the young policeman. "We could've questioned him."

Behind Mike the full moon hung fat and low on the horizon, illuminating an irregular patch inside the jail where she stood glaring at the young man.

The policeman named Perry looked at her blankly. He wiped the palm of one hand on his pant leg, over and over, while the other nervously tapped the barrel of his gun against the other leg. It had been his first gun battle. He'd be jumpy for days.

Mike sighed, then patted his back.

"It's too late now," she said. "Forget it."

Carter walked to her. Perry stared at him, miserable.

"The others disappear?" Carter asked.

She nodded. "Just stopped. They didn't get what they wanted."

"I'd better check outside," he said. "Come on, Perry. Let's see what we can find."

The young man stared at him, the pocks deep on his face in the gloom.

"When you're scared, it's better to do something," Carter said kindly. "You've got a bullet burn on your forehead. You've already been wounded. The worst is over. Don't you want to know where your chief is?"

The youth's eyebrows suddenly shot up. He crossed the room in long strides and exited through the hole in the jail wall where Carter had been.

Carter smiled briefly.

"I'll be back," he told Mike, leaving her to check the dead attacker on the jail floor.

He slipped past poor Harry and into the fresh night. The smell of gun smoke tainted the mountain air. Slowly the birds began to sing again. The tall firs swayed overhead with the singing wind.

Silently padding, gun safely in his hand, Carter moved around the perimeter of cleared land behind the rough jailhouse. Pine needles brushed his cheek. Dried duff softened the ground beneath his feet. He quickly found where the attackers had hidden during the last diversion. A thick log was piled high with branches. Behind it, grass was matted, duff kicked into piles where bodies had sprawled to fire at Mike and Perry.

He walked on, listening for human sounds in the forest. Altogether he found seven dead bodies, some close to the woods, others near the jail. They were dressed in black jump suits, Caucasians, their faces blackened for camouflage. All carried new Soviet 5.45mm AK-74 Kalashnikov assault rifles, smaller caliber versions of the traditional 7.62mm AK-47 model. The new models were light, tough, and easy to shoot, ideal for the Russian style of fighting that called for bursts of sustained fire rather than carefully aimed shots.

He returned to the jail. The lights were on once more. Villagers moved quietly toward the building, hesitant, not talking. Some carried hunting rifles.

Inside, Chief Merritt sat on a stool while a doctor tended a bullet wound on his arm. His leathery face was pasty, drawn. Villagers examined the blasted walls and conferred softly. Perry leaned against cell bars, his body stiff and wooden. A pall hung in the violated jail.

Mike had stripped the attacker that Perry had killed. He lay naked, pale as bleached bones, on the floor. He, too, had a Soviet gun. He also had a tattoo on the top of his left thigh. It was a small bird in flight. Beneath it were the Russian words *Serebryanyi Golub*, Silver Dove.

He struggled with the throttle. Sweat bathed his face. Slowly the nose rose. He steadied the throttle. It shook. His hands shook.

He couldn't turn the plane. They had to go straight ahead. Turning would make it lose all control, and spiral.

He watched the earth and aimed the plane for one of the gray strips of road below. Luckily the early morning hour was not a popular time for driving. The traffic was practically nonexistent.

Mike's knuckles whitened as she gripped the arms of her seat.

The flames whipped up over the nose.

Carter watched for traffic and for tall trees that could catch the light plane and tear it to shreds.

The ground rose to meet them at a dizzying speed.

Carter felt the blood drain from his face. His hands numbed on the throttle.

They had to get down fast, before the flames swallowed the engine. And the gas tank.

The plane bucked, fought.

The controls turned to mush.

But below, the dark gray road spread ahead like a welcome mat.

He pushed the sloppy throttle forward to land. Wheels squealed and bounced on the asphalt. No control. He pulled and yanked on the throttle.

The craft veered. With little air resistance, the flames erupted into the night sky. Heat shot up in the cabin.

The Cessna bounced into the tall roadside trees, flames crackling. The starboard wing ripped off. The plane dove into a thick stand of beeches. The impact threw Carter and Mike against the controls, the windshield, the seat, the ceiling.

The plane shuddered, then stopped. Flames roared. Heat stole the air from the cabin.

Carter shook his head, gasping. He ached all over. The heat was suffocating. The gas tank would go any minute.

"Mike!"

Her head lolled to the side, eyes closed. Unconscious.

He dragged her out, a dead weight.

He picked her up, threw her over his shoulder, and ran.

The thick forest of tall beeches stood silent and still, sentinels to the sudden explosion that rocked the land beneath Carter's running feet.

He fell with Mike to the ground, throwing himself over her to protect her.

The blast shot twisted metal and burning wood through the air. They were lethal missiles that could maim and kill.

Just as suddenly the air was quiet, unmoving. Heat spread thickly out to them from the fireball that had been a plane.

He rolled Mike over and felt for a pulse. It was regular and strong.

He carried her to the side of the highway, and sat for a moment beside her on the grass.

In the distance of the quiet farmland, cattle lowed nervously. Dogs barked. Sheep bleated. The land was rolling and grassy, with small stands of forest in the low places where water collected. He could see no houses.

Carter stood at the edge of the highway, waiting for a car. Behind him, the plane burned brilliant red and blue.

The first car slowed at the sight of the fire, then sped past Carter's waving arms, unwilling to be involved. When he heard the second car, Carter ran to the center of the lane, where he stood and waved. The car would have to run him down or go into the other lane and risk being hit by an oncoming vehicle.

It was a small Mazda, a sports model, bright yellow. Its tires screeched, and it angled sharply across the road to stop on the wrong side, opposite Mike and the direction it was heading.

"Nick!"

Mike was sitting up, groaning, holding her side. She fell back and screamed in pain.

He ran back to her.

"Oh, God, Nick!" she cried. "What happened! An accident?" She curled up on her other side.

"No accident," he said grimly, brushing the hair from her face. "Some kind of time explosive planted in your Cessna."

A first aid kit dropped at his feet, and a small CB radio. He looked up, but the gift-giver was already dashing back to the yellow Mazda.

"Hey!" he called. "Stop!"

But the figure slammed the Mazda door, and the car raced off into the night.

Carter opened the kit, found a flashlight, and turned it on. Mike was sooty, her face bruised. Gently he felt along her side. She bit her lip.

"Ribs, probably," he murmured.

"They hurt like hell," she said, tight with tension as she tried not to show the pain.

"They usually do. Not much I can do for you here. We'd better get you to a hospital," he said, turning on the radio.

FIVE

In Wellington, wind surfers sped across the harbor as the daybreak sun brushed streaks of yellow onto the gray sky. Crowds of barrel-chested men in shorts jogged determinedly into a pitched gale, getting fit for rugby, the national sport.

Tall palms snapped back and forth, hardy survivors in one of the windiest cities in the world. Wellington gets over a hundred days a year of winds greater than forty miles an hour. Citizens joke that they have to stake down even the cabbages and pumpkins that they grow in their backyard gardens.

Nick Carter thought about this as he rode along Highway 1, past the bay of Port Nicholson, toward the hospital in downtown Wellington that Mike Strange had specified. She lay uncomplaining in the back seat of the old Cadillac, her head in Carter's lap, her eyes closed. The inhabitants of Wellington—of all New Zealand—were known for their hardiness, and for their stoicism when faced with disaster.

The highway ended at the town hall, and the driver continued around the bay toward the center of the city.

"Sorry about the little lady," he said for the sixth time with his broad Midwest U.S.A. accent. He'd answered the SOS call first, an insomniac owner of a meat market— Harold's Butchery—whose nighttime avocation of radio listening either entertained him when he couldn't sleep, or—he

37

laughingly admitted—kept him awake long after he was relaxed enough to doze off.

"She'll be all right," Carter reassured Harold, and Mike, and himself.

"Broken ribs," Mike agreed, her eyes still closed. "I've had worse."

"One of the great things about New Zealand is the socialized medicine. You sick? The government picks up the tab," the driver went on, and snapped his fingers. "Came all the way from Chicago for paradise, and by God I found it!"

"Moved the Cadillac with you?" Carter asked.

"A beauty, right?" the driver Harold said. "A sixty-eight, and she's prime." He patted the dashboard. "Poor thing. She does have a nasty habit of collecting parking tickets. The Great Clobbering Machine—that's New Zealand's government to us—does have a few faults, but a clever fellow can get around them. Nonpunitive, you know. Half the time you get off."

"Ingenuity is admired here," Carter said.

The driver laughed.

"Don't I know it!" he chortled. "That's why I moved here. Paradise!"

The Wellington Hospital was not far from the Parliament building and the Beehive, the structure that housed the nation's government offices. Harold swung the Cadillac around to the emergency entrance, hopped out, and returned shortly with two men pushing a gurney.

"A chariot for you, little lady," he said grandly and pulled open the back door.

With old-fashioned courtesy, he escorted the group into the hospital, kissed Mike's cheek, took Carter to the admissions office, slapped Carter on the back in farewell, then disappeared like a spirit from another era out the door.

Astonished, the woman behind the desk stared quizzically after the vanishing man.

"Miss?" Carter said politely.

The pale room smelled of antiseptic. Metallic sounds, talk,

and rolling gurney wheels came from the hall. Several people waited nearby, some dozing in their chairs, others nervously turning pages in magazines they pretended to read.

The nurse looked at Carter, saw his dirty clothes, his sooty face, his disheveled hair, his too-short beard.

"What happened to the woman you brought in?" she said.

As he talked, she filled out forms.

"It will be a while," she said as she completed the last blank line. "One of the doctors will let you know."

He signed where she pointed.

"Sit with the others," she said. "It takes a while sometimes."

She gestured for Carter to take a chair with the group of discouraged, waiting people.

Instead he went to a telephone booth and made two calls: one to the AXE stringer in Wellington, the other to New Zealand intelligence.

Then he went outside and smoked.

The panel truck was painted white. The large black script said New Zealand Linen. Two men unloaded bundles wrapped in plastic and labeled sterile. Carter watched them work. They were efficient but slow. No one seemed to mind. They traded jokes with doctors and nurses. They were known and liked here. They carried bundles into the hospital, stacked them on a gurney, then returned for more bundles.

At last, the shorter man—swarthy with a handsome mustache that curled up at the ends—didn't return with the other. There was a difference of perhaps a minute, then he ran back out and joined his fellow worker.

Carter ground out his cigarette on the pavement and sauntered into the hospital toward the men's room. The nurse behind the admitting desk was busy with charts. The telephone rang. As she picked it up, Carter slipped into the men's room and locked the door.

There was a white, plastic-wrapped bundle on the back of the tank. He opened it. He took out the towel roller, fitted it into the towel case next to the sink, and pulled the white roll down so that it was within easy reach of any handwasher. He pulled out diversionary washcloths and pillowcases, and smiled. The Washington shipment had arrived.

He reached back into the plastic and picked up Wilhelmina, his remarkably accurate 9mm Luger. He balanced his old friend in his hand, then attached its holster at the small of his back and slipped the Luger in beneath his fishing vest. Suddenly he felt dressed.

Then he picked up Hugo, his pencil-thin stiletto, and slipped it from its special chamois case. The blade gleamed in the overhead light. He flipped Hugo into the air, and caught it in a neat slide back into its case. He attached the case to his right forearm so that at the twitch of a muscle Hugo would slip into his hand.

At last he picked up Pierre, his tiny gas bomb. He hefted it, and his fingers curled familiarly around it. The bomb snuggled in his palm perfectly. Hundreds of times Pierre had made Carter's escape from certain death possible. He attached the sphere high up on his inner thigh, where it fit like a third testicle.

In the mirror, Carter looked at his sooty face. He washed, brushed his fingers through his hair, and grinned. The vacation took on even more distance, but he would keep the beard until he had his time off.

He knew that to anyone else the only difference in him from when he entered the bathroom was that he was more tidy. But he felt an enormous difference—the physical presence of his old friends. They were a shield and an invitation. He thought of the assignment, of Blenkochev.

Again he reached into the plastic sack. He picked up a small radio that looked like a Sony Walkman and a wallet containing identification, cash, and credit cards. He walked out of the bathroom and closed the door.

"She's punctured a lung," the young woman doctor

explained to Carter. "A rib fragment. Not a big hole, you understand." Her voice was full of sympathy.

"She'll be up and around soon then."

"Yes. That's it," she said, grateful for his understanding. Even in paradise she'd had to tell too much bad news to too many loved ones. Now she was uneasy relating even an optimistic prognosis when she wasn't sure of the reception. She was still young; in ten years she'd either be hardened, or make grateful peace with her humanity.

"How long will she have to stay?" Carter asked.

The doctor smiled.

"If all goes well, only a week," she said. "She hurts more from the ribs than the lung, but the lung is what we've got to watch."

"I understand. May I see her?"

"Of course, but she's groggy from painkillers. She may not recognize you."

"I'll take the chance."

There were two guards outside Mike's hospital door. They were dressed in ordinary business suits, old and comfortable suits that complemented their casual slouches and disinterested faces. One or the other occasionally wandered up the hall, said hello in a hospital room, or talked to the volunteers who wheeled candy and good cheer along the antiseptic corridor. They were New Zealand intelligence, and they recognized Nick Carter.

"She's asleep, poor girl," the older one said. He had a talker's mouth and bright eyes. "Did give us a fright. I don't know whether to thank you for saving her, or knock your damned teeth in. If she'd died there, she wouldn't keep scaring our bloody wits away. Of course, then we'd lack for complaining, wouldn't we?"

He grinned charmingly, but worry hovered around the bright eyes. Whoever had set the explosives in Mike's Cessna might try to eliminate her again.

"She's lucky you're here to watch," Carter said and opened the door.

Both guards peered in around Carter, checked the room with hawk eyes, then nodded. He closed the door. Across the room, Mike lay small and unmoving on the narrow hospital bed.

Alone, he stood beside her, then took her hand. Intravenous tubes ran into her left arm. Her mass of chestnut hair spread out in a rich fan on the pillow. There was a pallor about her that made one think of death, but that was only the trauma of the injuries, Carter told himself. She would live.

"Nick." She smiled reassuringly. Then she frowned with thought, and took a breath. "I'm going to miss everything." Even in her weakened state she was indignant.

He chuckled. She was beautiful, talented, intelligent, and stubborn. Life was ten percent inspiration, ninety percent perspiration. Mike was a winner.

"Sorry," he said. "Looks like *you* get the vacation. I'll take notes and tell you all about it when it's over."

Her eyes snapped.

"I'll be out of here tomorrow!" she promised, then her face pinched with pain.

"Not tomorrow," he said quietly. "A week. And I don't want any of your magical escapes. Two of your friends are on the door. They'll keep anyone suspicious out . . . and, if they have to, they'll keep you in until the doctors say you can go."

"Some friends."

He laughed again. In three days she'd be plotting her escape. Within a day or two of that, depending on her strength, she'd be out. She was unstoppable.

"I've got to go, Mike. Sorry."

She looked at him balefully.

"Enjoy yourself," she said grumpily, then she smiled. "I'll be thinking of you. Care to kiss a fellow spy goodbye?"

* * *

Carter sat in the park near the hospital, the headphones of the small Sony look-alike over his ears. Lovers strolled nearby. Teen-agers laughed and giggled in the New Zealand summer sun. Children romped on the grass under the watchful eyes of mothers or older brothers and sisters. The traffic was moderate, slow as was the New Zealand habit. For a moment he thought he saw the yellow Mazda circling the park. A man in a tam-o'-shanter and small features was driving. It could have been the same one who'd left the first aid kit and radio after the Cessna's crash. No way to tell for sure.

Carter relaxed. He was just another park-goer enjoying the fresh air, warm sunshine, and a recording by the New Zealand Symphony. He pressed a corner of the machine. The music disappeared. A small keyboard slid out from the special AXE machine that used satellite electronics to hook into the mammoth AXE computer in Washington, D.C. He touched the buttons of the code he needed.

"Ah! Nick!" the sexy female voice whispered into his ears. "It's been too long. What can I do for you?"

Carter grinned and shook his head as he punched in his request. The sultry voice was one of Hawk's jokes.

"Rocky Diamond," the voice purred. She sounded like a cat who'd just licked clean a saucer of cream. "Real name Philip Shelton. An adventurer, born June 23, 1945, in Omaha. A graduate of the Air Force Academy, lowest marks in the class of 1967. Best known for his weekend passes. Put in his time with the Air Force, got out first chance he could.

"It was an honorable discharge," the husky female voice continued, "and few were sorry to see him leave. After that, he threw knives with a traveling Renaissance fair, punched cows in Wyoming, lived off a rich elderly widow in Los Angeles, and eventually drifted back to flying. His most recent work, as far as we can tell, has been for private contractors. He's 'for hire.' If there's a job that will pay him enough, he'll fly it.

"His character is unreliable, except where there's enough

money to stabilize him for the job. He does have one asset, however." There was a smile in the mechanical sex-kitten voice. "He's very attractive to women. His sex life is exhausting. His favorite drink is a martini with a dash of Pernod. Sometime in the last ten years he's affected an English accent and English ways, and lives accordingly. He's precisely six-one-and-a-half and weighs one-eighty-five. Sometimes his hair is brown, sometimes blond. Rangy, athletic, and smokes a pipe." The voice paused, almost breathless from its relating of important business matters. "Is there anything else, dear Nick?"

Carter stifled an impulse to thank the lifelike voice. Instead he grinned, pleased. Hawk had found enough information for him to begin the search.

Nick Carter thought about New Zealand as he rode the quiet elevator up through the warehouse building near the Rail Ferry Terminal. The nation was isolated geographically from the rest of the world, and that isolation had been turned by the citizens into an advantage. They'd created their own brand of civilization, one that pleased them and worked, despite similar controversial attempts that failed in Europe.

In the warehouse, the air smelled of dust, lumber, and oily machinery. On the first floor, room-size crates were piled so high that cranes were needed to unstack them. The elevator that Carter rode alone jerked. The cables groaned as it stopped.

He stepped off onto a plywood floor of a secret office whose location was described to him only after his second phone call to New Zealand intelligence. In a good organization, all contacts were checked thoroughly.

He walked across a narrow deserted hall. The automatic elevator door closed behind him. It was a typical warehouse room. Dust was puffed up in the corners. A single overhead lightbulb shed dim light. But he noted the hidden cameras, the size of U.S. nickels, embedded to look like knotholes in the rough lumber planks that served as walls. Probably some of the planks slid away so that hidden computer-controlled guns could swing out when needed.

He went to the only door. He spread his right hand on the shiny brown plaque that said Office. The plaque heated briefly. He took his hand away. The door swung open, and Colonel Chester ffolkes, chief of New Zealand intelligence, extended his hand.

SIX

The sounds of conversations, ringing telephones, and ratcheting computer printers swept through the open door into the small warehouse room where Nick Carter stood. Besides being skillfully hidden, the New Zealand intelligence headquarters were soundproofed behind the deceptive walls of rough planks.

Colonel Chester ffolkes cleared his throat. He was in his early sixties, a wiry man of medium height. His face was ruddy, his front teeth gold-capped. He had a hearty handshake, and a nonchalant gaze as his sharp eyes swept the empty warehouse room around Nick Carter.

"Sorry, old boy," he said to Carter as he drew the Killmaster over the threshold, enclosed the sounds once more behind the office door, and escorted the American agent down the tiled hall. "Would've liked to roll out the red carpet, but in our business . . . " He shrugged expressively.

"I understand," Carter said.

Maps and photographs of New Zealand lined the hall. Charts and lists hung nearby. A water fountain gurgled in a corner. The walls were painted a cheerful yellow. There seemed to be a half-dozen agents and secretaries at work, their desks in small cubicles piled with papers and books.

"Your superior, David Hawk, contacted me," the colonel said as he walked into a small office. He closed the door.

"Have a chair. Take the leather one there. It's most comfortable."

His appraising eyes watched Carter sit. Only then did he go behind his desk and settle himself in his wide chair. He was observing Carter, watching the fluid movements, the speedy physical reactions.

"I appreciate your seeing me on such short notice," Carter said. He took out his gold cigarette case. "Mind if I smoke?"

Again the gaze swept over Carter, pausing at the case. Colonel ffolkes allowed himself to smile. He knew he was being overly cautious, but then he'd lived a long time in a dangerous business. Caution was one of the prime ingredients to longevity.

"Delighted," ffolkes said. "May I?"

Carter offered him the open case, and the intelligence head chose one of the Killmaster's custom-made cigarettes. They were one of Carter's few affectations. Besides being made from specially selected tobaccos, each filter bore the initials NC embossed in gold.

With a flourish, ffolkes lit Carter's cigarette, and then his own. The New Zealand chief glanced briefly at the monogram. His eyes flickered with acknowledgment at the good taste of the agent sitting across from him, then he savored the tobacco.

The two men smoked quietly, each well aware that they were allies, yet the secretiveness of their jobs worked against their cooperating.

"How is she?" ffolkes asked.

Carter related the doctor's findings, then described his conversation with Mike herself.

ffolkes nodded, smiling.

"Good girl, that one," he said. "Wish I had a dozen like her."

"Any more information about Silver Dove?" Carter said.

"Still don't know whether it's a code, or whether it directly refers to a person, a place, or an organization. Your Hawk says Silver Dove is new to you, too."

"Whatever it is, it must be plenty big to bring Blenkochev out of Russia." There was something faintly familiar about the phrase Silver Dove. Perhaps from another operation . . . .

"Yes. Blenkochev."

ffolkes's ruddy face was a study in disinterest. He'd disciplined himself well. Still, the body sometimes betrayed the will. A vein on the intelligence chief's temple pulsed with agitation or excitement, or maybe both.

"You've met Blenkochev?" Carter said.

"I've had the misfortune," ffolkes admitted.

He drummed his fingers on the desk as memories flickered in his eyes. The disintegration began around the edges of the face. The muscles softened. Then he laughed, a series of mighty guffaws that broke his disciplined severity and re-sounded infectiously in the small room.

Carter smiled, waiting while the New Zealand chief wiped his eyes with a large white handkerchief.

"If he weren't so dangerous, I'd allow myself to enjoy him more often," ffolkes explained. He blew his nose, then stuffed the handkerchief back in his pocket.

"You were in the field with him too?" Carter said, stubbing out his cigarette.

"We all knew each other," ffolkes said and leaned back in his chair. "Hawk, Blenkochev, March from Scotland Yard, Parateau from Interpol, the others. Graduates of the secret services of World War Two." He took out one of his own cigarettes, and Carter lit it for him. "I was younger, had more to learn, and Blenkochev looked upon New Zealand as a potential Soviet ally. He took an interest in me. That was before Korea. Before the Cold War. Back when the Soviets were at least in name the friends that helped us win the war."

"That didn't last long."

"Interesting that we called it a world war. More accurate would have been a world *civil* war. One world, yet we all fought one another as if we were from different planets." The disciplined composure was coming back.

"And Blenkochev?"

ffolkes smiled. Laughter returned to his voice.

"He and Hawk were like two dogs after the same bitch in heat. Snarling and snapping at one another, but so busy pursuing the bitch that they didn't want to spare the time to fight a decisive battle. Their countries always came first. Yet, in their own ways, I think they liked one another. Maybe respected is a better word." ffolkes rolled the cigarette in the ashtray.

"What made me laugh was Blenkochev," he said. "One night on the Konigsallee in Düsseldorf, Blenkochev got drunk on beer. That in itself isn't remarkable, but you have to understand the kind of man we're talking about. This man carried a toothbrush even when he had to abandon everything else. He ordered his underwear starched. He read and reread Julius Caesar's famous battle campaigns. He was fastidious, meticulous, and his attention to detail made him a formidable enemy."

"Then he got drunk."

"Yes. He met German beer. He was a vodka drinker, of course, and vodka is so much stronger than any beer that he thought he could drink the beer like water. An enormous error. He ended the evening stripped to the waist, his pant legs rolled up, frolicking across the beer hall tables with pink-cheeked whores and waitresses."

Carter grinned, picturing in his mind the sight of stout, drab Blenkochev as a dancing maniac.

"Embarrassing," Carter said, "but not fatal."

"Then Blenkochev discovered there were photographs," ffolkes said, enjoying the memory of Blenkochev's tirade of horror. "And a German photographer who wouldn't be bought or threatened off. The photographer had survived the war. After that, even Blenkochev couldn't terrify him. Poor Blenkochev was beside himself. He could fulfill the most difficult assignment from Moscow—planting moles or arranging clueless assassinations—but he couldn't convince the photographer to not publish the photographs. And obviously he didn't dare kill him.''

"So?''

"The morning the photos were to appear in Düsseldorf, Blenkochev went to the newspaper building with a check for five hundred thousand Deutsche marks. He bought the newspaper on the spot, had the pressmen trash the edition, watched the head photographer destroy the prints and negatives, and then left town. As far as I know he's never been back.''

"I'm not surprised,'' Carter said.

"The newspaper went bankrupt shortly after. No one would run it. But there was never a word of complaint from Blenkochev. How or where he got the money no one knew. The rumors were that it came from profits on watered-down black market penicillin, but who knows? . . . The irony, of course, was that poor Blenkochev had betrayed his ideology. He'd been forced to use capitalist means to solve a question of ethics.'' ffolkes laughed merrily. "Poor Blenkochev. No matter how many times he would wash his hands, the stain would remain.''

"Reality is a tough teacher,'' Carter smilingly agreed, and lit another cigarette for himself.

"Don't get me wrong, Carter,'' the New Zealand intelligence leader went on thoughtfully. "I laugh at Blenkochev now only because he hasn't caused any trouble here . . . that we know of. He's about as friendly to the West as a pit viper is to a mouse, and as trustworthy. He has idiosyncrasies, but he uses them in his work. Perseverance. Ruthlessness. Cunning. I'd never want to face him off.''

"No one relishes that idea.''

"Then we understand one another,'' ffolkes said, again smiling. "And that brings us back to our business at hand.'' He blew a smoke ring into the air. His gold-capped teeth glowed in the fluorescent lighting. "And a simple question. Are you sure your missing American pilot exists?''

"Positive," Carter said, relating the information he'd received earlier that day from the AXE computer. "Some of his former employers have been putting pressure on Hawk to find him. Diamond's reliable when there's enough money involved, and these employers don't want to lose his valuable future services."

"They sound like illegal services to me."

It was Carter's turn to laugh.

"Probably," he said, "but now we're grateful because tracing him may lead us to why Silver Dove is important, and what caused the earthquake that jarred Blenkochev loose from the Kremlin. Our sources are reliable. They're dead positive Diamond was in New Zealand, although they don't know what his job was, or for whom he was working."

ffolkes smoked reflectively.

"We have a major problem with following that up," he told Carter. "There are no records that show Philip Shelton, alias Rocky Diamond, ever arrived in or left New Zealand. No flight plans, no cargo manifests, nothing. As far as the official records go, we've never had a man by either of those names in our country. Just like the mysterious illness that killed the Russian attaché. We wouldn't have any evidence of that either except Mike and our doctors saw it with their own eyes. You don't have such a lucky break with Diamond. How do you plan to trace a nonexistent person?"

Carter smiled.

"If you know enough about someone," he said simply, "they always leave evidence of passage, no matter how hard they—or anyone else—tries to hide it."

Using one of his several identification cards with matching credit references, Carter checked into the Wellington Arms, a red-brick Victorian building with white gingerbread, located off Adelaide Road near the heart of downtown Wellington. He dropped his fortieth cigarette of the day into a flat box near the reception desk politely marked Smokers Please, pressed the foot lever, and the cigarette disappeared into a second level.

The clerk behind the desk smiled with appreciation, and gave Carter a fifth-floor room with a view of the Zoological Gardens.

Carter signed the registry, then slipped a twenty (New Zealand dollars) across the counter. The clerk stared at it, then at Carter. He was wary, but interested.

"Did you notice an American or Englishman come through here in the last couple of weeks?" Carter said casually. "A tall man, about my height. Rangy. English accent. Likes martinis with a dash of Pernod?"

The clerk's eager eyes dulled. He wouldn't get the extra money. He shook his head. He was honest.

"Popular with women," Carter added, smiling encouragement. "A real flamboyant type."

"Sorry, sir," the clerk said, disappointed. "I don't remember anyone like that, and I'm on duty every day just about."

Carter nodded. It'd be like hunting for one particular seashell on a Coney Island beach. Lousy odds.

"Take the money, son," Carter said. "Ask around. Maybe someone on another shift saw him."

The money disappeared into the clerk's pocket. A big smile appeared on his face. In socialized New Zealand, taxes were high. Tips were a hedge against inflation.

"Be glad to, sir," the clerk said, handing him his room key. "Anything I can do."

Carter left the hotel to go to a nearby men's shop to buy clothes. Without thinking about it, he automatically watched the streets for the bright yellow Mazda. Nothing. He went to a leather shop and bought a suitcase. Briefly he remembered the fishing gear that had burned to ashes in Mike's Cessna.

He shook his head, packed the suitcase, and returned to the hotel lobby. There'd been no sign of the Mazda. And no one seemed particularly interested in the short-bearded American tourist who'd just indulged himself in some fine New Zealand clothes.

In the lobby, Carter purchased a downtown map of Wellington, and a restaurant and touring guide. It had been thirty-six hours since he had last slept. Weariness dragged at him. He went upstairs to his room to plan his hunt for Rocky Diamond, shower, and sleep.

SEVEN

The names of the areas of Wellington reflected its Maori, English, and American past. Names like Khandallah, Ngaio, Crofton Downs, Kilbirnie, and Brooklyn were discouraging to Carter because they showed more than the past; they told of the present enormous size of Wellington. More than 300,000 inhabitants spread in an arc around the bay. And Carter needed to trace one single man, an outsider, who had no record of ever having been in New Zealand.

There was only one logical place to start: Wellington International Airport. He made a circle around the area, then consulted the restaurant and dining guide for bars.

In New Zealand, people drove on the left side of the road, mailboxes were painted royal red and shaped like dollhouses, and once every three years in the general election, prohibition was voted upon. It hadn't passed yet, but bar hours were commensurately short in a nation where the temperance movement could easily get out of hand. The bars closed at ten o'clock.

Nick Carter was mindful of this as he walked along Broadway, head bent against the howling wind, toward the Bayard Stockton Cellar. The international airport was south. Big planes roared in and out of the distance, lights flashing.

It was 6 P.M. The chilly Wellington gale slashed through

Carter's suit as if it were gauze. But Carter had slept, eaten a good meal, and was feeling fine, eager to discover what underlay the strange events in New Zealand.

Prepared, he wore his old friends Wilhelmina, Pierre, and Hugo. It was astounding what their presence did for the disposition of a Killmaster.

He pushed open the plastic-covered door to the Bayard Stockton Cellar. Cigarette smoke and stale liquor odors clotted the air. In the entryway was an enlarged color photograph of a sardonic man with red hair. Beneath the photo was typed the inscription ''Founded by radio announcer Bayard Stockton, the man with the golden-gravel voice, disappeared Christchurch on assignment, July 1984.'' The photo and inscription were covered with clear plastic thumb-tacked to the wall. Carter shook his head, and walked down four cellar steps. Not your usual high-class establishment.

The bar was dark, the only light coming from small bulbs hidden behind cheap bloodred lampshades. The wallpaper was red, too, and heavily flocked. Four people sat at the bar, empty stools between each. They'd staked their claims to isolation. Behind the bar was a large painted canvas, a poorly done imitation Modigliani nude. The bar had aspirations. It wanted to grow up to be a whorehouse.

Carter sat on a stool at the end of the bar and loosened his tie. The heater was on. Even in summer, Wellington nights could be cold. His face flushed with warmth and stale air. The bartender looked at him.

''Lion beer,'' Carter said.

The barkeep nodded, picked up a glass, and slid it beneath the tap. As the beer poured, Carter took in his fellow drinkers: two women, two men.

Each of the men glanced at Carter, furtive, polite. The women stared down into their drinks. Not often in this country did you see women alone in a bar. And they weren't soliciting, just drinking. One had a whiskey sour, and the other a rum and cola. They didn't look like Rocky Diamond's types.

The bartender watched Carter study the women.

The beer came down hard in front of Carter. It sloshed over the side of the mug. The women looked up.

"Nice night," Carter observed, smiling curiously at the surly bartender.

"You looking for someone?" the bartender demanded.

He had brutal eyes, a short pugnacious nose, and cauliflower ears. He'd never been to the Olympics, just on streetcorners with too much time on his hands and no common sense. Now he was older and knew better, but he wouldn't pass up a challenge he could create.

"As a matter of fact, I am," Carter said.

"You won't find her here," the bartender said.

The barkeep had it all figured out. In New Zealand, a lady was to be protected. Unlike the United States where the indentifying line between lady and streetwalker was blurred by sometimes indistinguishable dress, in New Zealand a whore looked like a tart, and a lady looked like someone's mother. The two women at the bar were either mothers, or wanted to be. Their brows were raised in alarm.

"Your sister?" Carter asked, glancing at the closest of the two women.

"Cousin," the bartender said gruffly. "Drink your beer and get out."

Carter put a twenty on the bar. The bartender was good at jumping to conclusions. Maybe he'd jump a different way if the motivation changed.

The bartender's hand came down on the twenty.

But before he could slide the bill away to the cash drawer, Carter's hand came down hard on top. Surprised, the bartender flinched and tried to pull the money and his hand out from under.

The hand was immobilized.

The barkeep's eyes narrowed. He thought about the situation, his brow wrinkled with effort.

With his free hand, Carter casually picked up his beer and drank.

Again the bartender tried to yank away, but Carter's steely muscles held the fighter to the spot.

Carter put his beer mug down.

"I said I was looking for someone," he said.

"So?"

The bartender wouldn't concede an iota. But his hand had started to sweat. He made occasional furtive attempts to regain his dignity by slipping away.

The four people at the bar stared, not quite sure what was going on.

The bartender knew. He'd played games of intimidation before, his cagey eyes said, but he'd always made sure he had the right role—the bully's role.

"An American flyer," Carter went on. "When he talks, he sounds English."

The bartender licked his lips. Mesmerized, he watched Carter's free hand play easily with his beer, as if there were no strain involved in keeping the New Zealander pinned.

A flush of worry rose up the bartender's bull neck. Even though he used the excuse, he didn't fight for women, honor, or patriotism. He fought because he expected to win. The destruction of others proved that he was real.

"Already got too many bloody Americans around here," the bartender growled.

"English accent," Carter repeated. "Tall man, about my size. Rangy. Likes martinis with a dash of Pernod. Also likes the ladies." Carter nodded politely at the two staring women at the bar. They'd have a fresh story to tell their less venturesome friends, this one about a bearded, uppity Yank. "Sorry, but he's got a big reputation. Very successful at picking women up and getting them to bed. Name's Rocky Diamond." He smiled at the bartender. "I want to find this man," he said pointedly.

The bartender shrugged.

Carter ground the hand painfully into the counter. The bartender tried to bite back a grunt of pain.

"I'd appreciate any leads you can give me," Carter told

him. "Either to him, or to someone who saw or knows him."

The bartender clenched his teeth.

"Never heard of him," he hissed.

Then the bartender's hand lashed out. It was a scarred hand, marked by battles more often won than lost.

Carter sighed.

He smashed his free hand into the bartender's jaw. It was a single, perfect punch.

The fighter's eyes widened with surprise. Blood dribbled from the corner of his mouth. The beaten bartender crashed back into the Modigliani nude. Bottles of bourbon, rum, and gin smashed to the floor. Flying glass embedded itself into the cheap oil painting.

The barkeep sat down abruptly in the middle of the mess. He fell back against the collapsed liquor shelves. His head, framed by the cauliflower ears, drooped to his chest.

Fascinated, the patrons leaned over the bar to watch as the unconscious man slowly keeled over. His head landed on an unbroken bottle of crème de menthe. He seemed to smile.

Still leaning over, the four turned their faces to look at Carter. They sat back on their stools.

"Any of you see Rocky Diamond? Hear anything about him?" Carter asked.

They shook their heads.

"Don't recognize the name," one man said.

"A lot of tourists here," the other added.

"Sorry," the woman who was the cousin said. Then she smiled. Slightly, but still a smile. She hadn't liked the cousin much either.

Carter grinned. He drained his beer.

"I'll be at the Wellington Arms if you hear anything." He gave them the name he'd registered under.

The bartender on the floor moaned. No one looked.

Carter reknotted his tie.

"What about the money?" the first male patron asked, glancing at the bar.

Carter put another twenty on top of the first.

"Tell him to get boxing lessons."

The wind was a howling gale through the Wellington night. The stars were hidden behind a furling layer of gray and charcoal clouds.

Over the next several hours Carter worked his chilly way up and down Broadway and its sidestreets, going from bar to bar. He ordered a beer at every stop, but finished none of them. He needed to be alert.

It was at times like this that he wished he had a force of agents at his disposal. Or at least an assistant. Anyone to help share the legwork of giving the simple description, and asking the simple question, Have you seen or heard of this man?

His feet were growing numb from the nighttime cold. His nose was frosty. He was again feeling his lack of sleep, but still he persevered through the windy night.

Often a mission was lost simply because of poor footwork. Answers seldom arrived on silver platters. Most often they had to be dug out with a seasoned trowel.

The bartenders, waitresses, and patrons he approached in the Wellington bars and restaurants around the airport tended to be suspicious and closemouthed. Part of it was his scruffy beard. But mostly it was the standard—and normal— reaction.

So, consequently, each time he had to find what would loosen their tongues—bribery, sympathy, coercion, or some- times, for a lonely drinker, a friendly chat.

The questioning took time, energy, and money, and he was running low on all three. And no one he talked with had met or heard of Rocky Diamond.

It was a half hour before closing time, and Carter ducked his head to reenter the wind-blasted night. The bar he was leaving was the Plow and Angel. The one he would go to next was the Moon Face, two doors away.

His leather-soled shoes snapped on the cold pavement. He

dug his hands deep into his jacket pockets and hunched his shoulders as the wind pummeled him down the empty sidewalk. Most Wellington citizens had enough sense to be home on a night like this. And to think it was summer.

There was an alley to his left. A black rectangular hole. He rushed past, propelled by the gale.

Still, with his peripheral vision, he saw the momentary flash of the knife's blade within the blackness of the alley's entrance.

He kept moving. Only one more store, a jewelry shop with hand-hammered gold and silver necklaces displayed in the window, then he'd be at the next bar. The Moon Face.

Whoever was in the alley would have to be a lot quicker if he expected to catch someone to rob on this windy night.

Then he heard the feet.

They ran out of the alley, thundering. Ten of them. Dressed in black jump suits. Their faces darkened against the city's lights. Dressed and camouflaged just like the group that had attacked the mountain jail.

Carter grabbed Wilhelmina from the small of his back.

One of them lunged at Carter's legs.

He kicked him off.

They circled.

Carter spun, swinging the Luger.

He caught another one in the neck. His hand was so cold that he hardly felt the violent blow.

The man's eyes rolled up into his head, and he went down uncomplainingly.

But the others attacked, a circle of determination.

Too many. They could afford to have reflexes a little slower than the Killmaster's.

They came in high and low.

Carter lashed with his gun, his elbows, hands, and feet.

It was like fighting an avalanche.

He kneed one in the belly. The attacker doubled over and vomited.

He whipped another across the cheek. The black makeup

scraped off a fish-belly-white face that quickly turned red with blood.

They grabbed his arms. Ripped Wilhelmina from his hand. Pinned him against a brick wall. There were too many of them.

Quickly before he broke free, one belted him in the jaw. Another blasted two hard punches to the spleen.

Red and black pain erupted behind Carter's eyes.

"Forget Diamond!" one man snarled.

It was a low voice. Rusty, disguised. English, but a Russian accent.

"What?" He wanted to hear the voice again.

"Go home!" rasped another.

They were black wraiths in the night. Each looked like the other. Thin-lipped carbon copies wearing black jump suits padded against the wind. They had revolvers strapped to their legs. They worked in unison, well trained and enthusiastic.

"Silver Dove!" Carter said.

That did it. With machine-gun repetition, the fists hit Carter's face, neck, chest, and belly. Over and over. Punishing him for his knowledge.

He struggled.

They hit harder, an exploding series of pains that left him gasping against the rough brick wall.

"Don't try to follow Diamond!" a new voice warned, finality in the words. "Next time, you're dead!"

To emphasize the point, another attacker grabbed Carter's head and slammed it back into the brick wall.

Hands released Carter. He slid down, every muscle in his body screaming. Warm, sticky blood oozed from the back of his head. The Wellington street revolved crazily. He felt the faintness of the few seconds before unconsciousness.

The attackers stared at him solemnly.

Silently they turned and ran down the deserted street.

The night's chilly cold radiated from the sidewalk. Carter awoke in the brittle stillness of it, knowing he should get up, knowing he'd be stiff, maybe even ill and out of action if he didn't.

Couples hurried past him, sneers in their voices as they circled distastefully away. They thought he was a drunk, or a deadbeat, or maybe worse. A few cars passed, their bright lights sweeping the sidewalk. Music and laughter blared out onto the sidewalk as up and down the street bars and restaurant doors occasionally opened and closed.

Carter stood up. A wave of nausea washed over him. With shaky hands, he dusted uselessly at his jacket. He grabbed for the wall to steady himself.

As another car slowly drove up the street, he stepped into the alleyway. There he found Wilhelmina in an inky shadow. He dropped the Luger into his jacket pocket and stumbled back to the lighted sidewalk. The beating had been expert, designed so the body would not forget.

He patted his pockets for a cigarette. The car was small, yellow. The nausea returned, this time accompanied by faintness. His knees turned to water, but his mind still worked.

The yellow car was a Mazda, and it had slowed to a crawl in front of him.

Suddenly the knees buckled. Dizziness engulfed him. He forgot the cigarette and the yellow Mazda. Once more he fell unconscious to the cold sidewalk.

When he awoke, he was troubled by dreams of being dragged. They were indistinct dreams complicated by his being cozily back in his hotel room bed, the sun shining bright and innocent through the window, and bandages and assorted smelly ointments covering parts of his body.

Gingerly, he stretched. Felt the sore muscles ripple. The pain made him smile. He was alive at least. He moved his bones and joints. Nothing broken.

He flung back the covers and sat up. Nude, he walked carefully, and then with more confidence, to the bathroom. He relieved himself, then stared into the mirror. White bandages made a patchwork of his bearded face. He pulled the bandages off. Abrasions and cuts, but nothing serious. He returned to his bedside table to check his watch.

It was eleven forty-five. He'd slept a long time, maybe twelve hours. What was necessary to revive his battered body. When professionals go to work on you, recovery isn't fast or easy, but it helps to be in the extraordinarily trained condition of a Killmaster. He looked around the room. His closet was open, the clothes from last night neatly hung. He picked up the telephone.

"Yes, sir?" the clerk from yesterday said from downstairs.

"Any messages for me?"

"I'll check."

There was a moment of silence, then the eager young man was back.

"Nothing, sir. Sorry."

"Did a man driving a yellow Mazda bring me in last night?"

"As a matter of fact, my coworker did mention that. A pleasant fellow. Helped you to your room. Called the hotel doctor."

"Any name? I'd like to thank him."

"No, sir. Said he was just a samaritan. You'd been attacked by one of the rough waterfront gangs."

Carter sighed. The samaritan was obviously the man in the yellow Mazda. That's where the dragging part of his dream had come from.

As if in a haze he remembered being hauled to his feet and half dragged, half pulled to the small car. He remembered the door's banging shut, opening his mouth to thank his benefactor, then passing out again.

The stranger was a real puzzle, impossible to identify at this point. Carter had never had a good look at the man's face. He didn't know age or even hair color because the man wore the tam-o'-shanter low to the ears. Didn't know the car's license plate. Didn't know why—or whether—the stranger was following him.

"Anything else?"

"Well . . . there is one more thing. But I don't know whether it's still important . . ."

"Rocky Diamond?" Carter said, suddenly alert.

"It's not much," the young clerk warned, "but I remembered what you said about asking around, and one of the maids said she'd seen a man like you described. He came in drunk with a woman to visit one of our guests. He ordered martinis with a dash of Pernod at the bar. The maid didn't remember which guest they were visiting. Anyway, they laughed all across the lobby to the elevator. Very undignified, she thought."

"Did the maid hear him say anything?"

"Christchurch," the hotel clerk said, pleased that he could deliver information to a guest who paid so generously. Money may not buy love, but it regularly buys cooperation. "He mentioned Christchurch. The woman hung on his arm and begged him to take her along, too."

Carter grinned.

"I'll be damned," he said.

EIGHT

Consistent with a city founded by nineteenth-century English gentlemen, Christchurch was tweedy rather than trendy. Formal flower gardens decorated the manor houses of the rich, while tidy flower beds of snapdragons and posies dotted working class bungalows. Storybook swans swam in streams and ponds. Picture-postcard schoolchildren wore loden green blazers and carried traditional field hockey sticks.

Christchurch's pace was slow, almost casual. It was a reflection of upbringing that emphasized good taste, not how many cars were sold today, not how much money would be made tomorrow. Business flourished without frenzy. Financial success was admired but not flaunted in the most English city outside Great Britain.

Nick Carter thought about this as he spent the next two days quietly working his way across the city of more than 300,000. There were more restaurants than bars. Christchurch was a city of shopkeepers, all with small eccentricities in the English way to set their establishments apart.

He went to Grimsby's Restaurant housed in a converted medieval-style church. To the gaudy Shangri-La, which promised in plastic what the movies had provided in celluloid. To the Oxford Victualling Company decorated with old wooden booths and iron gooseneck lamps. To the

Waimairi Lounge where young marrieds on the way up talked rugby and politics. And to various Chinese, Mexican, Italian, American, English, German, and any other kind of ethnic bar or restaurant the fertile mind can contrive.

It made him tired and gave him indigestion, but he continued. Even in a city of 300,000 individualists, Carter knew that it was only a matter of time until perseverance would pay off. With luck.

It was dusk of the second day. Rosy-cheeked youngsters of European descent rode bicycles through Christchurch's Cathedral Square.

The town hall and the Anglican cathedral dominated the parklike area. Seagulls circled and called overhead. Unemployed teen-age Maori boys stood on the corner, their shoulders hunched, smoking cigarettes. Their dark Polynesian faces with the handsome flat bones were sullen and discouraged in the fading light. All was not perfect in this English-inspired paradise.

Carter strode past them, past the square, past the Savoy Hotel to continue his methodical search. He wore a Fleet Street suit imported from London and a jaunty attitude that covered his growing discouragement. His beard was beginning to look like the affectation of a monied businessman rather than the sloppiness of a penniless derelict.

The next stop was the Wyndham Club, a posh three-story hotel hewn of fieldstone. There were heavy brocaded drapes at the arched windows and an obsolete footman at the front door. The footman bowed and touched the brim of his cap as Carter mounted the steps. Proper clothes and the right attitude bought you respect, if not peace of mind.

The smells of expensive whiskey, brandy, port, and old wood perfumed the air of the first-floor paneled bar. The bartender wiped a white cloth across the shining bar and smiled appraisingly at Carter.

"London?" he asked.

Carter stood at the bar, put a foot up on the rail, and nodded.

"Just got in."

Tell a person what they expect to hear, and you confirm their intelligence. Instant rapport.

"Went to London once," the bartender went on.

He had pale blue eyes and thin silvery hair swept back close to his head. His dignified posture suited the hushed bar.

"Did you like it?"

"I was disappointed, sir. I'd expected the fogs. You know, the thick pea-soup fogs of Sherlock Holmes and Jack the Ripper?" The bartender of the high-class establishment had a taste for adventure. "But when I got there, they told me that the fog was really smog, just air pollution, and that London had new ordinances against it. There hadn't been a thick pea-souper since the sixties. Very disappointing."

"I can imagine," Carter said.

The bartender stopped polishing and looked at his only customer.

"What would you like to drink, sir?"

"Martini with a dash of Pernod."

"Unusual drink," the bartender said as he went to work.

"Serve it to anyone else lately?"

"No, sir."

The barkeep dropped ice cubes into the shaker one at a time, clinking. He poured in Boodles gin, nipping up the mouth of the bottle at just the right moment. His hands moved with the flourish and drama of a concert pianist. He held up a bottle of Cinzano vermouth.

"Twelve to one?" he asked.

"That's it," Carter nodded, continued. "He would've been a tall man, rangy. About my size. English accent. A pilot."

The silvery-haired bartender worked without pause. He added the quality vermouth and stirred the mixture cold. He splashed Pernod into a stemmed glass, poured in the martini, twisted a lemon peel over it, and with a flick of the fingers dropped the peel into the concoction.

He stood back, crossed his arms. He was a general awaiting the outcome of an important battle.

Carter sipped thoughtfully.

"Excellent," he announced. "Tender, not bruised."

The bartender beamed. Carter had made his day.

To show his appreciation, Carter drank.

As he cleaned up, the bartender watched his customer enjoy the fruits of his talent.

"You have a new bottle of Pernod, I see," Carter said at last.

The bartender hesitated, and looked at the bottle as he returned it to its shelf.

"Indeed. We don't open bottles often. Even in the summer."

Pernod was a summer drink, usually served over shaved ice. Green from the bottle, it turned milky yellow when it hit the ice. The liquor was prized for its faint licorice flavor.

"Wonder who had the last drink from it," Carter said casually.

The bartender said nothing. He mopped the bar. He rinsed glasses. He dusted bottles.

"You could call," Carter suggested, sipping. "Ask them."

The bartender who enjoyed his work but still yearned for the adventures of Sherlock Holmes's London fogs nodded, took off his apron, and left the room.

Carter hoped that this was the luck he'd been waiting for.

The bartender was phoning his fellow Wyndham bartenders to inquire whether any gentleman lately had asked for a martini with a dash of Pernod.

He was gone twenty minutes. When he returned, Carter had finished the martini.

"An interesting situation," the bartender confided as he retied the apron.

Carter waited patiently. It was the bartender's moment of

glory. Still, he had the urge to throttle him. It'd been a long two days.

"You had success?" he asked.

"I believe so," the bartender said solemnly. "There was a gentleman here, a guest of the hotel, named Shelton Philips. Handsome man. Even dashing, or so the ladies seemed to think."

Carter smiled. Rocky Diamond's birth name was Philip Shelton.

"Last week?" Carter said. "Do you still have the charge slips?"

"His room, sir. Of course you'd want that."

The obliging bartender went through the bar's copy of receipts. When luck happened, it was often abundant. But while you're doggedly, hopelessly pursuing elusive information, you forgot that.

The room number was 203.

When Nick Carter stuffed twenty dollars in her pocket, the second-floor maid of the Wyndham Club remembered Shelton Philips.

Philips was still renting the expensive room, she recalled. She was a short brunette with bright eyes and a mobile mouth. He'd paid up until next week.

With another twenty dollars, the maid unlocked the door, blew Carter a kiss, and disappeared to assault the next room with lemon wax.

Rocky Diamond's room at the Wyndham Club was decorated with hand-painted china plates, brass fixtures, heavy mahogany furniture, a hardwood floor, and a hand-knotted Oriental rug that started just inside the door and extended the length of the oblong room to beneath the high four-poster bed.

Rocky Diamond liked to spend money. Was it his . . . or someone else's?

Carter started with the drawers in the bureau, found the usual assortment of socks, underwear, and handkerchiefs.

The closet contained two business suits—a dark blue and a gray pin-striped—and shoes and leisure clothes.

Wherever Diamond had gone, he hadn't taken much with him. An austerity trip, or perhaps he'd simply been kidnapped, killed, and his body chopped into shark bait.

Carter checked the linings and pockets of the clothes, tipped over and shook the shoes, then went through the rest of the drawers in the room.

He found Wyndham Club stationery, a Gideon's Bible, a woman's brassiere and bikini underpants, tissues, and a case of men's jewelry. He worked with precision, carefully replacing everything as he'd found it.

But his luck had run out again. There were no financial records. No checkbooks, credit cards, or even local shop receipts or matchbooks.

It was almost as if Diamond had expected his room to be searched. His belongings were personal but revealed nothing of his true identity or his intentions in Christchurch or New Zealand.

Except that he planned to return.

With practiced eyes, Carter's gaze swept the room. What had he not checked?

The walls, ceiling, and floor.

Again he went to work, checking behind and beneath the furniture, the floor heater, the floor of the closet, under the rug, the plates behind the light fixtures, the vent grate. Nothing.

Then he heard the sound at the door.

A small sound, trying to be silent.

There were no other doors. Carter was trapped.

Swiftly he crossed the room and pushed up the window.

There was a narrow ledge, about twenty-four inches wide, and then the two-story drop straight down.

Not an enormous distance, but enough to break a leg . . . or a spine. And there were no fall-breaking awnings or trees between him and the concrete below.

Carter slipped out the window and onto the ledge. Beneath

him, pedestrians window-shopped and cars spumed exhaust into the air.

With luck, no one would notice him, would call him to the attention of others, to the attention of the police. Or Silver Dove.

As he closed the window, the door to the hotel room opened and closed.

The man was slight, quick. He slid skeleton keys back into his pants pocket.

Carter smiled to himself. In a way, he'd been expecting him.

It was the same man who'd left the CB radio and first aid kit for Mike on North Island. The same man who'd returned Carter to his hotel in Wellington after the attack by the Russians. The man who drove the yellow Mazda, wore the tam-o'-shanter cap pulled low to his ears, and had small features.

His movements were careful, experienced. He followed a similar pattern of search to Carter's. He wasn't looking for Carter this time, and he wasn't a burglar. He was a professional agent.

Carter watched from high up in the window, his feet firmly planted on the two-foot-wide ledge. His body was out of sight. Only his head could be seen, if the other agent were quick enough.

Wind whistled around him. Periodically he ducked out of view as the searcher, growing frustrated, would stop to survey the room and think.

It was at one of those times that Carter's own gaze saw the scrap of paper. It was a piece of notepaper, folded small to fit in a wallet or key case, resting at the top of the bottom pane of windowglass inside the room. It could easily have dropped when two hands—rather than the expected single hand— were required to reach up to unlock the double-paned window. (It was a stiff window.) And the scrap would go unnoticed by maids who cleaned only what was visible.

Carter smiled broadly, patient as the agent completed his

methodical search of the room. The man spent a good hour at it, even removing the plates that covered the light switches and electrical outlets. He was after Rocky Diamond too. But what was his reason . . . and for whom was he working?

At last, discouraged and disgusted, the agent pressed his ear against the door. When the sounds outside told him it was safe, he opened the door and slipped out.

Carter reopened his window, grabbed the folded paper, and followed.

The agent strolled past the House of Natural Health Foods Sanatorium, the New Market Butchery, Reynolds Chemists, Woolworth's Variety, and back into Christchurch's Cathedral Square.

He was a slender man wearing nubby tan slacks, a London Fog windbreaker, and the jaunty tam-o'-shanter. He strolled with his hands in his pockets, his shoulders relaxed, giving no indication he was concerned about being followed. That in itself was enough to make Carter suspicious.

An agent as good as this one appeared to be would be crossing streets, dipping in and out of stores, backtracking—because if he's on an assignment, he's a marked man. By somebody he often doesn't know.

He's also always on the lookout for unusual amounts of interest in him or what he's doing. That could lead him to information he needs. With Carter, careful use of a city's streets was second nature. Seldom was he tailed without his knowledge. He'd lost at least one tail in Christchurch yesterday. And two in Wellington. Part of the job.

As they entered the square, Carter hung back farther.

The strange agent blended in with the European New Zealanders, his very English clothes like the very English clothes of the other inhabitants in the square.

Carter had never heard the stranger's voice, wondered whether there'd be a Scotch accent to fit the tam-o'-shanter, or another accent—Eastern European, American, Russian—that the tam-o'-shanter was worn to deflect.

The agent turned toward the flower stand in front of the big brick and stone post office. He had a strange gait, very idiosyncratic. If Carter had enough time to study it . . . .

Instead, Carter ambled off, apparently heading for the men's rest room.

The agent selected a bouquet of yellow, white, and blue daisies from the flower woman. It was a simple, conversation-filled transaction, and Carter scanned the square, bored.

Until he saw Blenkochev.

The chief of the dreaded K-GOL was coming through the big double doors of the post office as casually as if it were the Kremlin.

The old agent was dressed in a dowdy, rumpled suit. Very English. He was shuffling through a stack of overseas envelopes as if looking for a remittance check.

It was a good cover, and Blenkochev was hardly recognizable as the polished Soviet official in Mike's photograph.

He was there to meet the man in the tam-o'-shanter.

Despite the enormity of the implications of having the world's top KGB man working once again in the field, Carter had to smile.

Blenkochev was good. The hands trembled ever so slightly. The nose was made up floridly red to suggest too much drink. And then just the right touch—the look of need on Blenkochev's face brightened into greed when he found the right envelope and ripped it open. He beamed as he read the amount on the fake check. Then he walked as if looking for a bar.

Meanwhile, the young agent in the tam-o'-shanter was busying himself at the flower stand, still engaging the flower woman in small talk. As the agent watched Blenkochev from the corner of his eye, he rotated the bouquet in his hand, cradled it a moment in his arms, then dropped it to his side to tap it against his thigh. He didn't know what to do with the thing.

At last, finishing the chat, the young man said thank you and turned.

Bumped into Blenkochev.

The envelopes flew into the air.

The bouquet dropped.

Both men bent to retrieve their belongings, and Carter saw the brief conversation that occurred without either man actually looking at the other. The young agent was reporting in, Carter lip-read. The old agent was disgusted with the message, then issued orders. They exchanged no looks or packages.

The two stood, shook hands, once again polite strangers. Apologies were given.

They walked off in directions ninety degrees apart.

Carter followed Blenkochev, giving him plenty of room.

Blenkochev walked at a brisk pace through the square, circled back, took advantage of the men's rest room, paused on a park bench to rest, then ambled around the post office to the street.

At some point he'd spotted Carter. But the AXE agent stayed with him. The KGB man didn't try very hard to lose the Killmaster.

Back at the street, the yellow Mazda was at the curb, and Blenkochev strode toward it. His too-long suit jacket flapped against the baggy pants.

The young agent reached across the front seat and opened Blenkochev's door. Impatient, he gunned the motor.

Blenkochev hopped in, turned, and looked back through the window.

As the Mazda sped away, the old fox gave Carter a small, impish smile and a tiny wave. It was a salute, one pro to another.

Grinning, Carter watched the Mazda weave into the Christchurch traffic. There was no point in following Blenkochev. Carter had found what Blenkochev had sent the young agent in the tam-o'-shanter for.

He took the small folded notepaper from his pocket, opened it, reread the address, and hailed a taxi.

● ● ●

Carter's destination was southwest, beyond Christchurch's city limits, in a sparsely populated area near Wigram Aerodrome. Willows and oaks dotted the dry landscape. Abandoned farm implements were rusty reminders of the original purpose the English gentlemen had had in mind for the land.

Now the area was partitioned into vacant lots, waiting for sale or foreclosure. A Maori family stood on a sagging porch as Carter drove by in the rented car. They were quiet people, exhausted by life. They didn't wave, but they watched Carter turn down the road that led to Charlie Smith-deal's address. His passing was their day's entertainment.

Carter parked the rented car in the shade of a willow whose branches brushed the ground. The summer afternoon had grown hot; it was almost eighty degrees. New Zealand's weather was not only dramatic, it was unpredictable.

He got out of the car and looked around. Smith-deal's house was little more than a shack. Tin cans, tires, a roll of barbed wire jumbled on the ground around it. Weeds sprouted limp from thirst. A metal flap from a broken reaper banged as a light breeze stirred dust into the air. It had been a good, sturdy house once. The foundation was even of stone. A dirt trail led to the sagging front porch. Carter walked up it.

He knocked.

"Smith-deal!"

No answer. He knocked again, called again, circled around to the back. No one there either.

He returned to the front, his hand on the doorknob, when he saw the old jeep lurching along the country road toward the shack.

The driver was having trouble deciding whether he preferred the accelerator or the brake. The vehicle would rush forward, skid almost to a stop, then would leap ahead like a jackrabbit with a shotgun at its tail.

Carter watched the jeep's erratic progress and smiled.

When the jeep at last ground to a dusty stop in the jumbled yard, he walked toward it.

"Charlie Smith-deal?"

"Betcha!" the driver said, exhaling a cloud of whiskey. His eyes were red and bleary. He jerked his baseball cap around so the flap was over the back of his neck. He raised his foot, aimed it outside the jeep, and set it deliberately on the ground. He grinned at Carter.

"Do I know you?"

"Don't think so," Carter said, grabbing Smith-deal's arm to steady him.

He followed Smith-deal up the path to the shack's porch. Smith-deal never wavered, a dog on a scent. There was probably a bottle in the shack.

"I'm looking for a friend," Carter went on. "Name's Rocky Diamond. You might know him as Philip Shelton, or Shelton Philips."

"Oh?" Smith-deal's interest was waning. He opened the door. "Need a drink."

There was a faint, plastic click.

Carter tackled Smith-deal's legs. Hurled them off the porch. Rolled them next to the stone foundation.

The shack exploded.

NINE

The ground shook and rolled. The roar of the explosion rocked their eardrums. Dust and debris clotted the air, and the two men huddled next to the stone foundation and coughed.

The bomb had been set on a split-second delay switch to be sure that anyone entering would be inside when the explosives blasted the shack apart. That had been the soft click that Nick Carter's acute hearing had picked up. Just like all experts, bomb professionals tried to think of every contingency.

As Carter picked up Charlie Smith-deal and held him by a wobbly shoulder, he thought about it. Too much of anything was often not a good idea . . . even too much efficiency.

Smith-deal gazed at the stone foundation of his shack, now filled like a volcano crater with wood splinters useful only to a toothpick factory. Dust settled slowly toward the ground.

"Shit," he said mournfully.

"Sorry about that," Carter said. "Looks like somebody doesn't like you. You'll need a new house."

"Never mind the bloody house!" Smith-deal cried in outrage. "Me bottle was in it!"

"I *am* sorry." Carter grinned. "You don't have an emergency bottle, maybe? Hidden somewhere?"

Smith-deal looked blankly at Carter. Slowly memory brightened his eyes. He snapped his fingers.

"Dammee, you're right!"

Carter followed Smith-deal across the jumbled yard to the back. The drunk went straight to a well with a low stone wall. The overhead arch that had held a bucket was long gone. The bucket was nearby, upside down, with a tattered rope tied to the handle. Smith-deal ignored it. Instead, he pulled up a second rope that was fixed to a deeply embedded hook inside the well's wall. The bucket was left outside the well so that the puller wouldn't get the ropes confused in the night.

Carter looked over the well's edge into darkness. Slowly the jug appeared. It was home-brew in a plastic bleach bottle, not an encouraging container. It had been there so long that algae covered it in a slimy green.

Smith-deal crowed with pleasure. He sank next to the well, his back supported by the wall, lifted the bottle, and drank.

Carter squatted next to him.

"Looks like you've been having a good time," he observed. "A long celebration of something."

"Can't figure it," Smith-deal said, wiping a fist across his mouth. "Who'd want to blow the old shack? I don't even own it."

"They were after you, not the shack."

"Doesn't make a goddamned bit of sense."

Smith-deal drank again, long and deep. At last he sighed, and set the jug next to him. He kept a proprietary arm around it.

"You don't want any, do you?" he inquired.

"Wouldn't dream of depriving you," Carter said.

Smith-deal beamed and rotated his baseball cap so that the brim was again over his eyes, sheltering his face from the afternoon sun. He was in his early forties, a slender man in need of a shave. What flesh he had was pulpy, almost without substance. He'd been drinking for years and not bothering to eat when he did. He appreciated those who didn't take the liquor that he substituted for proper nourishment.

"It's not all that great," the New Zealander admitted and drank again. "But you can have some. Sure. You saved my life. I think. Didn't you?"

Carter laughed.

"Probably, but you keep your booze. Instead, maybe you'd answer some questions. Know anything about airplanes?"

Smith-deal blinked slowly, digesting Carter's words.

"Mechanic," he replied, still puzzled.

"Know a flyer by the name of Rocky Diamond?"

Smith-deal hooted and slapped his thigh.

"Oh, he's a hard case, he is!" he said. "One of the hardest cases around!"

"Did you see him last week?"

The mechanic's eyebrows knitted in thought. His forehead creased with suspicion.

"Why d'you want to know?"

"If I wanted to hurt him, I wouldn't be bothering to talk to you now. I'd have you down, your arm locked back, and your neck stretched from here to Auckland. You'd tell me anything I wanted."

Smith-deal blanched.

"Diamond's missing," Carter continued. "Maybe he's dead. Maybe he's hurt somewhere and needs help. If he's your friend, you'll want to tell me what you know."

Smith-deal drank, then looked at Carter with bleary eyes.

"He flew out of Christchurch?" Carter prodded.

"That's it," the mechanic said. "Don't know whether he'd want me to tell you or not. But then, if the poor boy's missing . . ." He shrugged. "Ah, well. He should be there by now, and no damage done. He was doing a bet. Someone hired him to make a stunt flight from Christchurch to the South Pole. He was supposed to stay overnight there and then fly on to the Falklands. When he took off, he gave me a wad of money for helping him and to keep my mouth shut. I went off to celebrate. Haven't been home since." He stared mournfully across the yard to the remains of the shack.

"It saved your life," Carter reminded him. "If you'd come back sooner, you wouldn't have heard the click and you'd be dead."

"Don't know why anybody'd want to kill me." The mechanic shook his head sadly. Thinking about it was upsetting, so he drank again.

"Did he file a flight plan?" Carter went on.

"Sure. Had to. Everyone does."

"And he had plenty of supplies?"

"Everything. Snow equipment mostly. Just in case. Food, too, and survival gear. No frills. And the gas tanks were full. Saw to it myself."

"There's no record of him at either Christchurch International Airport or Wigram Aerodrome."

"Well, we were quiet about it all. Rocky called himself something else—Philip something—but there should be records. The flight plan."

Carter stood and dusted his hands.

"Come on," he said. "There's someone you need to talk to."

He lifted Charlie Smith-deal by the armpits and steadied him on his feet. The mechanic clasped the algae-covered jug to his chest.

Smith-deal was the only witness Carter had to Rocky Diamond's presence in New Zealand. Smith-deal believed what Diamond had told him, but somewhere in the man's unconscious there might be clues about what Diamond had really been up to. Carter would get Smith-deal to Colonel ffolkes and let the New Zealand intelligence head's expert psychologists take over.

"Not sure I like this," Smith-deal muttered as Carter propelled him around the house.

"Can't be helped," Carter said, aiming him at the Ford Laser 1.3 he'd rented in downtown Christchurch. "No one's going to hurt you. Just help you remember better. Might actually be fun for you. Interesting."

"Don't like this at all!"

Smith-deal wouldn't be convinced easily. Alcoholics didn't like change. The most important constant in their lives was threatened—liquor.

Still, Carter urged him toward the Ford. And Smith-deal, whose will had long ago evaporated in an alcoholic haze, went.

The bullet streaked through the sunlight.

Instantly the AXE agent dived. He yanked Smith-deal down and pulled out Wilhelmina.

The bullet bit into the ground five inches from Carter.

Carter dragged Smith-deal with him to shelter behind the rented car.

Smith-deal quaked. His teeth chattered as he gripped the plastic bottle of booze to his chest.

The whining of two more bullets split the air. They were high-pitched screamers from a long-range rifle. The sharpshooter—or sharpshooters—were trying to draw Carter and Smith-deal out from the car.

"W-what's going on now?" Smith-deal yelled.

"You got a gun in your jeep?" Carter asked.

"An old hunting rifle, but—"

"Back seat? Front seat?"

"Under the front seat, but—"

"Don't move," Carter ordered, "or you're dead!"

Smith-deal nodded solemnly, his ashen face registering that once more he'd had a foot in the grave.

Carter looked across at the battered, muddy jeep. It was twenty feet away. The air was silent, the rifleman or riflemen saving bullets, waiting for targets.

As Smith-deal unscrewed his bottle, Carter dashed for the jeep.

A bullet ripped through the jeep's hood.

"Hey!" Smith-deal yelled. "That's my jeep!"

It was dirty and banged up, but—unlike the shack—it was his. Ownership was more important than safety.

"Smith-deal! Get down!" Carter shouted.

Confused, the mechanic ducked as another bullet whistled over the Ford where Smith-deal's head had been a moment before.

Because of the time between shots, Carter knew it was one

rifleman. Before the sharpshooter could resight, Carter vaulted into the jeep's front seat. He pulled out the old rifle and a cardboard box of bullets. Now he had to get out again.

"Smith-deal!" Carter called. "You still got that jug?"

"Yeah!"

"Take a drink and hold it high so I can see it!"

Obediently, the mechanic swigged deeply and lifted the big white bottle above his head, above the hood of the Ford.

"Steady!" Carter urged.

"How come?"

The answer came in the whine of a well-placed bullet.

It burst the big plastic bottle. Liquor sprayed into the air, dousing the Ford and Smith-deal's face. Pieces of plastic fell to the ground.

"No!" cried Smith-deal.

He pulled the handle down and stared at it as if by his needs he could reassemble the bottle. Tears ran down his cheeks, and he licked the inside of the handle.

Again using the brief time before resighting, Carter leaped over the jeep's door and sprinted to the Ford.

"Why'd you have me do that?" Smith-deal complained. "I oughta knock your head off!"

Angry, the drunk wiped his arm across his eyes. Anger was what Carter needed, not submersion in the immobility of self-pity. An angry Smith-deal was useful, perhaps useful enough to save his own life and help Carter capture the sharpshooter.

"Here," Carter said, and he shoved the rifle and ammunition at Smith-deal. "There's only one over there. Behind the trees on that knoll. Keep him occupied, but don't get yourself shot."

Smith-deal frowned. His eyes narrowed. He was beginning to get the idea.

"Can you handle it?" Carter said, checking Wilhelmina's chambers.

"You're going after him?"

"You have a better idea?"

"We could just drive out of here."

"He'd get the tires, the gas tank."

"It'd be safer."

Carter laughed. "You mean it might get you closer to another drink."

Smith-deal drew himself up where he squatted in the dirt. "Nothing wrong with a man having a drink now and then."

"Nothing wrong at all," Carter agreed. "Afterward, I'll buy you one myself. Whatever you want."

"I want a bottle. The best Irish."

"You can count on it."

Carter slapped Smith-deal on the back and crawled to the end of the car. It'd been a long time since the last shot.

"He may move," Carter warned Smith-deal over his shoulder. "Be careful."

Smith-deal raised his baseball cap, scratched his scalp, and flopped the cap back onto his head.

"Got it," he said, and lifted the barrel of the rifle over the hood of the car.

Instantly another shot rang out, landing in a blast of dust a few feet behind the car.

"Guess he's watching me," the drunk said worriedly.

"Good," Carter said, and ran.

Slowly Carter made his way around the gently rolling, sparsely settled plain. In a country where hunting was one way a family kept from starving, there wasn't any noticeable excitement about the rifleman on the low knoll who kept Smith-deal pinned down and tried to stop Carter in his speedy dashes from one shelter to the next.

The rifleman had lost the advantage that came with surprise. He was a good shot, though, and persistent. Eventually, if he wasn't caught or didn't give up or didn't run out of ammunition, he'd get one or both of his targets.

But he wasn't a professional killer.

A professional would have disappeared after the first miss. He would have escaped—unnamed—to succeed the next time.

Carter needed to get in range for his 9mm Luger. He would wing the rifleman, rush him, and capture him. He hoped.

Once again Carter scrambled to his feet and tore across the hard plain.

Two bullets sang past.

He dived into a scrubby stand of oaks. Dry leaf dust puffed into the air.

He raised Wilhelmina. He was on the edge of being in range. He studied the hillock where the rifleman was hidden.

There a variety of trees presided over dry grass and downed logs. In the winter, the logs would be dragged away for firewood. But now they provided good shields for the rifleman.

Between Carter and the rifleman were no more shelters for Carter. Only the sun and the dirt of the open plain waited. If Carter couldn't get a good shot here, he'd have a long, dangerous run ahead. A run long enough to give the rifleman time to aim accurately for a kill.

Again Carter observed the knoll. The last place the man had fired from was to the left of a big maple, just above a thick log.

Carter lay still, watching.

Suddenly there was a shot from the Ford.

Charlie Smith-deal had remembered to use his hunting rifle. The bullet thudded harmlessly between two trees on the low hill.

A rifle barrel appeared on the hillock, in the place where Carter expected it. Quickly he aimed and fired.

The bullet was short, the distance still too great.

Carter ducked.

Immediately a bullet streaked past him.

Smith-deal fired again, his whiskey-riddled mind fixed on the promised bottle.

Again the rifleman shot at Smith-deal behind the Ford, and Carter raced away from the stand of trees into the open plain, shelterless and dangerous.

The voice was hollow, almost like a cough. It seemed to be calling Carter's name.

The bullets blasted from the hillock, one at a time, steady, now ignoring Smith-deal behind the Ford.

Carter weaved. The voice coughed again.

The sharpshooter's shots were closing in. Carter zigzagged.

The bullet ripped through Carter's sleeve, burning his skin.

The next one might kill him, and yet he was almost at the knoll.

"Carter!" the voice said.

As the rifle on the hillock barked again, Carter rolled.

The bullet sang into the dirt.

"Over here, Carter!"

Carter rolled again, this time into a narrow trench, invisible from any distance on the gently rolling plain.

"Colonel ffolkes," Carter said and grinned. "I was just on my way to call you."

"You're a damned hard man to follow," ffolkes said, his ruddy face pressed against the side of the dry irrigation trench. His gold-capped teeth shone in the sunlight.

"You're the one I lost in Wellington and then Christ-church."

"A couple of my men. You didn't think we'd let you run around without being watched, did you?"

"Considering the present situation, I can hardly complain."

The two agents shook hands.

"You have any more men here?" Carter said.

"A few," he said modestly.

The operation was simple. Carter, Colonel ffolkes, and the three New Zealand agents who were stationed nearby rushed the hillock from different directions.

The sharpshooter fired quickly.

The men pressed on, themselves firing on the lone rifleman, racing at him. A converging juggernaut.

Until there was silence.

An unnatural silence.

Carter put on a burst of speed, ffolkes close behind. Even though ffolkes was in his sixties, he was in excellent shape. His wiry frame ate the ground in long strides.

They found the sharpshooter crumpled behind the log that had sheltered him. Half his face was gone. The powder burns were unmistakable. Suicide.

Despite the years of experience, both Carter and ffolkes hesitated. Suicide was somehow more a tragedy than even murder. It made each man question his own pain.

Then, as the other agents arrived, ffolkes went through the dead man's pockets, but he found nothing.

Carter watched until ffolkes was finished. Then he unzipped the man's trousers and pulled them down. The White Dove tattoo was on the corpse's left thigh.

TEN

The tea was hot and delicious—Lapsang Souchong by Twinings, "Teamen to Connoisseurs for over 275 Years." A very English blend with the heavy, smoky flavor of burnt tar, probably discovered when tea leaves were thoughtlessly stored on tarred ropes in the belly of some four-rigger sailing ship. Instead of being horrified, the clever merchant advertised the tea as the newest taste from the Orient. And the English, with their tolerance and appetite for the unusual, loved it.

Nick Carter drank the tea with milk and sugar, the way fine black China tea should be drunk. And the way Colonel ffolkes took his.

The colonel put his cup down on the scarred coffee table next to the report. Weariness showed on the deepened lines of his face.

"Rocky Diamond didn't arrive in the Falklands," ffolkes said, tapping the report. "We've checked the mechanic's story front to back, and most of what he says appears to be true. Near as we can tell, Diamond took off Wednesday last week, planning to camp overnight at the South Pole and then fly on to Stanley in the Falklands. Mackenzie—an old friend of Diamond's—knew about it. Too bad he did. Meant his death. Anyway, your Yank carried no illegal cargo, only his personal supplies. As you know, New Zealand's roughly at a

hundred-seventy degrees east longitude and the Falklands are
at sixty degrees west, so it was close to a straight-across-
the-Pole trip. Barring weather and acts of God, it should have
been easy. But something happened, and the poor bloke
never arrived.''

"And his employers?"

"No employers. Smith-deal was wrong about that. It was
personal. The bet was with one of Diamond's old pilot rivals
in Stanley. Very macho, as you Yanks say. And for a lot of
money, which the cocky bastard fully expected to win. The
rival was beginning to hope that Diamond had backed out.
Bit of a pleasant surprise when we told him Diamond was
missing.''

Carter and the New Zealand secret service head were
sitting alone in a small storage shack not far from the United
States' Deep Freeze Base at Christchurch's airport. Air conditioning hummed, both relieving the end of the hot day and
camouflaging their voices from inquisitive ears.

The windowless shack was stacked with wood storage
crates at the end nearest the door. A passageway that weaved
among the tall stacks of boxes led to the small sitting area at
the back where Carter and ffolkes consulted. It was furnished
with folding chairs, an overhead fluorescent light, an
apartment-size refrigerator, a hot plate, and a coffee table
scarred by cigarette burns, coffee rings, and the scuff marks
of hard-heeled boots.

Outside, the surrounding complex of buildings housed
offices and storage for the U.S. Navy and the National
Science Foundation personnel who supported Deep Freeze
operations on Antarctica. They were the link between life and
certain frozen death for the isolated stations on the great
wasteland.

The services were basic—housekeeping, food, clothing,
medical aid, mail communications—and originated from the
headquarters in Port Hueneme, California. They were implemented in the busy Deep Freeze complex at Christchurch.

The busyness was what had attracted ffolkes to the area. A

windowless shack and innocent neighbors helped to maintain the secrecy of his operation.

"And the rifleman?" Carter said, sipping his tea. "He was a sleeper?"

"Exactly," ffolkes said, nodding. "A New Zealander of Russian descent. Second generation. No police record, never in any trouble with the law. Just an ordinary working bloke waiting to perform the one crucial act that would reveal him as an undercover agent for a foreign group."

"What kind of working man?"

"Personnel director for a big sheep processing company."

"Any trouble there?"

The colonel picked up the report and read. As he turned the first page, Carter could see the big red stamp that said Most Secret.

"He was reprimanded twice for complaints of racial discrimination," ffolkes said thoughtfully. "Maoris weren't being hired, and the few who were weren't being promoted to management jobs."

"After the second complaint, he improved the situation just enough to quiet the protestors," Carter said.

"That's it," ffolkes said, picking up his cup. "The complaints mean something to you?"

"Perhaps," Carter said. "I'd like to contact Hawk. See what he has to say."

"Of course," the colonel said and stood up. "I'll be waiting."

"Nice to hear from you, Nick! Do you by chance know what time it is?"

"Two A.M. there, I believe, sir."

There was a long pause. Carter settled back in comfort to wait for Hawk to clear the sleep from his brain.

The Killmaster was calling from the back seat of a VIP limousine he'd found on a quiet sidestreet near the Deep Freeze Base. He'd seen the U.S. general go up the front steps of the house, hat in hand, and the chauffeur go around to the back. The men had been there before, and each knew where to find his entertainment.

Carter had glanced up and down the street, then picked the limousine's lock and slipped into the back seat. The car smelled of wool uniforms and oiled leather. The windows were tinted so that passengers could see out while outsiders couldn't see in. It was a comfortable, relatively safe place for Carter to call his superior on the small Sony-size radio.

At last in far-off Washington the butane lighter clicked. There was a sudden gust of air as Hawk's cigar came to life.

Hawk sighed and puffed in the distance.

"Very well, N3," he said. "Let's have it."

Carter reported the events that had taken place since Wellington, including the strange inhabitant of the yellow Mazda meeting Blenkochev in Christchurch's Cathedral Square.

Hawk was silent.

"Interesting how the past is always with us," he said at last. "I thought those days were behind me. I even allowed myself to be nostalgic for them. The good old days. But the reality is that nothing's changed. Blenkochev and I have been at war since before 1949 when Mao took over China."

"That's a long time."

"Our countries have beliefs that threaten the other. There's nothing to be done. Blenkochev and I must continue to try to outwit, outmaneuver, and outkill one another. That can only stop when our countries no longer perceive the other as mortal—and moral—dangers. And now we have Silver Dove to further irritate the elements."

"Then you think I'm right, sir?"

"Naturally," Hawk said gruffly. It might be the middle of the night, but he was still in top form. "Silver Dove . . . Knights of the White Camelia . . . the White League . . . the Pale Faces . . . all names for various versions of the Ku Klux Klan in the 1860s. I should've made the connection before. An organization that started as a social club and grew into one of the strongest underground hatred movements in the world."

"The name Silver Dove seemed familiar to me, too," Carter said, "but I didn't put it together until Colonel ffolkes mentioned the protests against the sleeper's racist personnel policies."

"We're getting somewhere at last," Hawk mused, puffing on his cigar. "Good work, N3. *Serebryani Golub*—Silver Dove. Russia's modern version of racial and moral supremacy. I'll check it out. Meanwhile, our most direct link is obviously the missing flyer Rocky Diamond. We must find out what that Russian group is doing. You'll of course retrace Diamond's flight."

"It'll have to be a guess, sir. The flight plan is still missing. Colonel ffolkes suspects that the Soviet sleeper used connections to find it. And then destroyed it."

"Unfortunate," Hawk said, not surprised. In espionage, a well-placed sleeper has years to develop the connections and skills necessary to accomplish any task. "Don't forget warm clothes, N3. Better yet, I'll come down there and see that you're outfitted properly."

"Sir?" Hawk had many facets, but this sudden motherliness startled Carter.

"Blenkochev is in New Zealand." Hawk's voice was impatient again . . . and full of vigor. "Do you expect me to stay behind a desk in Washington?"

Carter lit one of his cigarettes in the back seat of the limo and smiled. It would be a difficult but interesting hunt.

Colonel ffolkes's wiry body was sprawled on the floor next to the scarred coffee table. Carter checked the room, then knelt beside him. Unconsciousness had turned the New Zealander's ruddy face ashen. The china teapot was shattered. The colonel's folding chair was knocked onto its side.

The secret report of Charlie Smith-deal's testimony, Rocky Diamond's flight, and the sleeper's background lay on the intelligence chief's chest. It had been tossed or dropped there.

Someone else now knew that Rocky Diamond's destination had been the South Pole and Stanley.

Carter considered this new piece of information as he lifted the colonel's eyelids and checked his pulse. The colonel's heartbeat was strong and regular. A lump the size of a goose egg had formed on the back of his head. Carter wet his handkerchief and wiped the unconscious man's face.

When the secret service director's eyes fluttered, Carter spoke gently.

"Did you see them?" he asked.

"Dammee, no," ffolkes replied. His hand reached toward the lump. "Sneaked up on me. But it was only one. Light-footed. Here." He unfolded the fingers on the other hand. An ordinary olive-green button lay on the palm. "Guess I still have a bit of the old agent in me."

Carter picked up the button. It had only two holes.

"Mind if I keep it a while?"

"It's the least I can do." Colonel ffolkes smiled wryly.

ELEVEN

The nuclear submarine skimmed just beneath the surface of the Pacific. Wind-blown and chilled from his ride in the open trawler, Carter watched the crewmen work and listened to the hollow sound of conversation, the bleeping sonar, and the quiet clicking of computerized equipment as he followed the lieutenant through the smoothly efficient work area and down a narrow corridor.

"Can you swim?" the pale lieutenant asked Carter cheerfully as they walked.

"Some."

"Don't ask for a submarine assignment then," the lieutenant advised. "It's a wasted skill. We go down, doesn't matter whether you're wearing pajamas or a wetsuit, you won't have a chance to swim for it. Not a damned thing you can do."

"Except make sure it doesn't happen in the first place."

"That's it," the lieutenant said and beamed. He liked the challenge of his job.

"Career Navy?" Carter asked.

"Is there any other way?"

David Hawk, chief of AXE, was waiting in a cloud of cigar smoke in small private sleeping quarters. Air conditioning sucked futilely at the gray haze.

"It's about time, Nick," Hawk growled. "Come in. You'll have to sit on the bunk. Good God, you've grown a beard!"

The AXE director nodded a silent dismissal at the young lieutenant. The lieutenant saluted smartly and closed the door.

"Good officer," Hawk said, then turned his attention to Carter. "You'll be glad for that beard where you're going. We've got a fine mess on our hands with this Silver Dove business."

David Hawk had the kind of nondescript wide face and stocky body that lent itself well to disguise and adaptation. He was of medium height, the still-strong muscles not obvious under his three-piece Washington suit. Only the muscles in his forceful jaw showed as he worked on his cigar. His only outstanding feature was a shock of white hair.

With padding, he could be disguised as a well-to-do European businessman. With the right kind of loose clothes, he could be a down-and-out vagrant. With makeup, tinted lenses, and dyed hair, he could blend into almost any culture. He could do those things even today. Instantly.

He had been a chameleon as a field agent. And now, in his sixties, as he smoked his cigar in the small submarine cubicle, Nick Carter had the feeling that the AXE director wanted that again.

For the moment, Hawk once more wanted to be the premier Killmaster. The best agent, not the best agency head. He didn't want to be the mastermind sending Carter or someone else out to do the job. He wanted to do the job himself. He wanted to take on Blenkochev, and settle once and for all his superiority in the war of wits and nerve.

"There's a communications flurry from Soviet embassies all over the world to the Kremlin," Hawk said grimly.

He sat at the small desk, his face stern and impassive. He exuded power like a woman does perfume. The power came from deep within him, honed by experience and intellect. It was so much a part of him that he was unaware of it. But anyone nearby felt it like a cold wind.

"What are they saying?" Carter asked.

"We haven't broken the code yet. They're using top

emergency communications. Reserved only for worst-case situations . . . such as war.''

"Silver Dove?" Carter said from the bunk, and lit a cigarette.

"There's nothing else unusual going on. It's got to be Silver Dove they're talking about. Right now we're assuming the Dove group is one of the KGB's 'unofficial' terrorist organizations. I have people in Moscow checking it out.''

"What does Silver Dove have to do with Rocky Diamond and the dead embassy attaché in Wellington?"

Hawk allowed himself a brief smile.

"That's your assignment, Nick," Hawk said. "Find out what Silver Dove is doing. And that means the Antarctic. By backchecking, we've discovered that the 'business' trip the Soviet attaché was on included Paris, Rome, Moscow, Hong Kong, Sydney, and somewhere in Antarctica before he returned to the embassy. Antarctica wasn't scheduled. We think that whatever's going on down there is influencing the Soviet uproar.''

"I see.''

"I thought you might.'' Hawk puffed thoughtfully on his cigar. "Silver Dove appears to be a large organization. And old and well established enough to have at least one sleeper agent who waited for his assignment a good fifteen years. It wouldn't be unusual for an embassy to not know about one of the KGB's undergroups. When their attaché died, they acted innocently to save him. And then Blenkochev arrived, and he hasn't gone home. Something is happening with Silver Dove that he has to direct or keep on top of.''

"Something that has other Soviet embassies interested,'' Carter said. "Or worried.''

"That's right,'' Hawk said, the cigar in his mouth. The noxious gray cloud increased.

"And what will you do, sir?''

Hawk glared at Carter. The AXE chief stood, walked three paces across the room, turned, and retraced his steps. His teeth clamped the cigar. His hands knotted behind his back.

He walked back and forth like a caged tiger. A powerful caged tiger.

"Wait. Watch," the AXE director said. "This isn't the only operation I've got. I have people on assignment in the Middle East, Berlin, Beirut, Central and South America, South Africa, you name it. Anything could blow up. Right now the Antarctic business is the most active, the most crucial. And with Blenkochev here . . . well, you know about that. But meanwhile, I've got a brigade of people out there trying to cap volcanoes of potential violence. What else can I do?"

"You could go into the field with me."

Hawk stopped pacing. He looked at Carter. He pulled the cigar out of his mouth, studied it, and jammed it back in.

"It's what I want, of course," he said quietly.

"There'd be two of us. A better chance at success."

Hawk was silent, his steely eyes suddenly taking on a wistful glow. He looked around the small white room.

The sleeping quarters where Carter and Hawk met belonged to an officer with a wife and two young daughters. The family picture sat on a low shelf above the desk. The blond officer in dress whites, the wife in a summer dress that showed good shoulders and a sunny disposition, and the daughters in starched pinafores over frilly dresses. It was a smiling, happy family, holding hands, the girls each on a parent's lap. The best of us. What freedom was all about.

Hawk's chin jutted with determination.

"You have your job," he said gruffly. "I have mine."

"And Blenkochev?"

"Blenkochev's a damned fool. Always was. Conniving and shrewd, but given to extremes. My guess is that he's working that man in the Mazda, using him as his direct assistant. Just because Blenkochev is out in the field neglecting everything else is no reason for me to. But then he's got a bureaucracy sixteen layers deep that will keep his operation going."

"What tempts you is that you know him better than any of us."

Hawk allowed himself a smile of acknowledgment. Carter understood.

"A conceit on my part, I suppose," the powerful AXE chief admitted. "The greatest adversary I ever had. Wily as a fox. Totally amoral. What's he up to? It's enough to tempt me into stupidity. You're the only agent I trust to take him on, Nick. Blenkochev was never too proud to get help even from despicable sources. Silver Dove isn't my idea of a group with a good cause. They're bigots. They draw members from Russians who constantly push the Communist ideology against religions of all kinds—particularly Jews. Speaking out against religious practice isn't enough for them. They bomb churches, cathedrals, and synagogues. They kill religious leaders. Those in positions of power won't let Jews emigrate. Instead they throw them into prisons and 'hospitals' where they are tortured. It's one thing to be an atheist. It's something else entirely to hate people who have a god just because they have a god. And then you add their poisonous attitudes toward different races—blacks, Orientals, whatever—and women . . . and you have a really swell group of supporters."

"Or employees."

"Yes. Employees."

Hawk sat again in the chair by the desk. He waved a hand absently through the cigar smoke and laid the foul-smelling cigar butt in an ashtray to die a natural death.

The ventilation system worked doggedly on the close atmosphere. The small living quarters with the bright white walls was gloomy not only with smoke, but with the two men's thoughts.

"We can't make the world better until people's inner lives are ruled by love and compassion, not fear and hate," Carter observed.

"People can't make themselves better until countries encourage understanding and appreciation among one another. They've got to realize that national fears and hatreds lead ultimately only to destruction. And if governments are designed as well to guarantee a man or woman's basic needs, then individuals can develop themselves and their potential to the highest level.''

Carter ground out his cigarette. The men stood. The submarine would surface soon.

''I suppose the answer,'' Carter said, ''is that both have to happen simultaneously. Individuals and nations striving for the best together.''

''And meanwhile,'' Hawk added, ''we have work to do.''

Carter nodded, then held the door for the older man.

''Blenkochev and Silver Dove,'' Carter said.

Flat-topped icebergs glowed eerily blue in the choppy South Pacific. They drifted past the submarine like fat elegant matrons on the way to the bank.

It was summer in Antarctica, January, a time of around-the-clock sunlight and the pulsing activity of an international array of scientists studying winds, rock formations, tectonic movement, sea life, ocean currents, glaciation, and human nature.

McMurdo Station was not far ahead, just beyond Ross Sea and McMurdo Sound. The U.S.-operated station would be Carter's jumping-off point. It was also the major Antarctic port for U.S. and New Zealand scientific activity.

He stood with Hawk, bundled in khaki-colored easy-movement fiberfilled clothes, joined by the captain and look-out on the submarine's bridge as they approached the world's southernmost land. Antarctica itself came from the Greek word *antarktikos*, which meant ''opposite the bear,'' the northern constellation.

The wind was brisk and sharp. Broad-winged skuas circled and dove for fish. Emperor penguins in their tuxedo disguises swam and played.

"A good day to arrive," Hawk observed, his eyes in binoculars scanning the white and gray land ahead.

"Hope it stays that way," the captain agreed as he, too, studied the Antarctic coast through binoculars. "Weather's changeable as hell."

Within an hour, the iceberg-clogged waters could alter from deep blue to silver to gray to black, and the sky from sapphire blue to a tempestuous white and charcoal life-threatening blizzard.

To the submarine's left loomed the vast Ross Ice Shelf, almost six hundred miles wide. It was bracketed on the far end by Little America and on this end by McMurdo Station, both operated by the United States.

To the right of McMurdo rose the rough, austere Queen Maud Mountains, as raw a range of rocky peaks as any on the globe. Carter would have to fly across them to reach the South Pole.

The submarine passed Cape Adare and a groaning glacial iceberg factory that casually calved chunks of ice the size of breadboxes and warehouses into the churning sea. They passed Ross Island where Mount Erebus stood in grandeur, one of the few continuously active volcanoes in Antarctica. And then, stars and stripes waving smartly overhead, the submarine came to port in McMurdo.

In the ice hut, Hawk spent the rest of the day overseeing Carter's outfitting. He selected the best and most recent equipment. Clothing, snow survival gear, processed food, and—most important—a small nuclear helicopter, large enough for only a pilot and passenger. With luck, the passenger would be a retrieved Rocky Diamond.

The two men packed the gear themselves, aware that a mistake—something lost, misplaced, or forgotten—could mean Carter's death. The AXE agent had not only Silver Dove and Blenkochev to contend with, but also the most relentlessly savage weather in the world.

Hawk posted a guard on the helicopter and gear it contained, then the two men ate dinner and found empty beds. They would arise in precisely eight hours.

During their time at the base, they'd found no one who'd seen or heard of Rocky Diamond.

Farther north, well above the Antarctic Circle, it was dawn. But at McMurdo Station in Antarctica where Carter and Hawk walked out toward the helicopter, it was just another ordinary hour in the continuous summer day. For two-thirds of the year, the continent at the bottom of the world was shut down and inaccessible—completely frozen in. The wasteland was so trapped in brutal snowstorms and endless night that even the native plant and sea life couldn't reproduce.

Carter considered this as around him in bright sunshine trucks rolled away from the station on ice roads, carrying wind machines in back. Scientists and construction workers in colorful snowsuits labored and shouted. Penguins, seals, and birds waddled and dived into the bay. In a wasteland, life flourished when it could. Nothing natural could stop life. Only the artificial, the man-made forces of holocaustal destruction could completely end life.

"All set?" Hawk asked.

He pulled the cigar from his mouth and stared south as if he could see the South Pole, Carter's only scheduled stop.

"Looks like it."

Carter got into the little nuclear helicopter. Ski marks in the packed snow behind it showed where it'd just been pushed from the storage shed. The man Hawk had entrusted to guard it moved quietly and tiredly away.

"You have four days," Hawk continued. "That's all. Your main supplies will last that long. Your emergencies should last two weeks more. I expect to hear from you every day. But I'll give you four, just in case. Then I send someone after you."

"I understand."

"No one's to know exactly what you're doing, so watch your radio transmissions."

Carter smiled. He'd never seen the great Hawk so worried.

"How'd you get out of that Ethiopian desert that Blenkochev left you in?" Carter asked as his eyes and fingers ran over the helicopter gauges. He glanced at Hawk.

Hawk was studying him, his eyes narrowed.

"How'd you hear about that? No, no. Never mind," he said and jammed the cigar back in his mouth. "A Bedouin found me. His wives took care of my wounds, and he gave me a lift on his camel to the Mediterranean."

"You make it sound easy. You were near death. How'd you get lucky enough to have a Bedouin find you? That desert's a thousand square uninhabited miles."

Hawk glared. He worked the cigar across his mouth.

"I took my watch apart," he said reluctantly, "crawled up the tallest dune I could find, and used the crystal to reflect light. I just kept shining it around until the Bedouin found me. I figured I was going to die anyway, might as well go with heat prostration. The chest wound would kill me soon anyway."

"Good thinking for a man near death."

Hawk shrugged. He allowed a smile to play on his lips.

"There are no Bedouins in the Antarctic," he warned. "Be careful." He stepped back. "And happy hunting!"

Carter closed the helicopter's plastic door and turned on the motor. He let it warm as Hawk stomped his feet and gusted cigar smoke into the pristine air. Hawk looked almost happy, as if he were sending a part of himself off with Carter, the best part, the part that longed for his own adventures again. Only once did Carter see him frown, and then the AXE head quickly covered it, a true professional.

The helicopter rose straight up, its rotors beating healthily. Skuas, Wilson's storm petrels, and snow petrels scattered away, their wings flapping into the brilliant sky.

Carter hovered the craft at about thirty feet. Abruptly Hawk raised a hand and waved. As Carter gave him a thumbs-up signal, Hawk nodded, clasped his hands behind his back, and stalked away. He had his own work to do.

In the helicopter, Carter moved across the Ross Ice Shelf, part of the ice sheet that covered the polar continent with as much as three vertical miles of ice. He watched for signs of a downed aircraft. The ice shelf was so vast that it contained more than seventy percent of the earth's supply of fresh water.

The cloudless day provided a clear view for about three hundred miles in all directions. Here and there sprouted remote scientific stations and temporary settlements of Antarctic Treaty member nations. The outposts were little cardboard boxes on the glistening snow and ice. But there were no wrecked planes. The treaty, due to be reviewed in 1991, made Antarctica an international haven for peaceful study, and the happy results of that were all Carter saw.

Carter thought about this as the small helicopter flew on toward Beardmore Glacier where he would fly over the jagged Queen Maud Mountains. Apparently it took the most undesirable piece of real estate in the world to be the spawning place for international peace.

In a few hours, as the day lengthened into afternoon, Carter at last reached Beardmore Glacier. Still no sign of Diamond's having passed there.

Ominous gray clouds billowed on the horizon. Antarctica's wildlife had disappeared. Seldom did even the thickly feathered petrels venture this far inland.

Beardmore Glacier extended ahead and up in shining blue-white glory. Here Edgar Evans, a member of Captain Robert Scott's ill-fated polar party, died in 1912 as the group of five men fought their way back toward bases that would eventually lead them to expedition headquarters at McMurdo Sound.

Carter pulled back on the throttle, and the helicopter rose, following the awesome glacier up between the sharp mountain peaks. Wide cracks marred the glacier, created by fissures below. He kept glancing at the weather gathering on the horizon and then down at the empty expanse of glacier.

He watched the sky. The clouds on the horizon were gathering force, splaying like knives across the heavens. He flew on, his attention divided between the land and the atmosphere. Only three hundred miles to his destination at the Pole.

The sky above Carter's helicopter was dark now, but he was almost over the glacier. He'd seen nothing of Diamond. The flatlands that contained the South Pole spread beyond the glacier. If he had to, he could tent the helicopter and wait out the storm at the Pole.

The helicopter suddenly rocked, knocked about like a leaf. Wind whipped viciously across the polar plain, hurling snow and ice into the air. The gray coulds released an ongoing burden of thick swirling snow. The air temperature plummeted, and the helicopter's windshield fogged. The radio went out, the victim of polar interference. A cold sweat broke out on Carter's forehead as he struggled with the helicopter's controls.

TWELVE

The Antarctic air was thick with snow. Visibility was nil. Nick Carter couldn't tell the dense snowy air from the polar cap below. It was a massive whiteout, and sky and land were the same. White death on white death. Indistinguishable.

He needed to land the helicopter. But he had to wait for a break in the weather so he could see.

Carter held the chopper steady as he could, the controls growing sluggish. Had a sudden storm taken Rocky Diamond, too?

The helicopter blew to one side, then the other. Up and down. Dizzying. Confusing. Without direction. While under the influence of the South Magnetic Pole, no compass was reliable.

For hours Carter rode the winds, waiting for a moment of visibility so he could land. He had to stay up; he could not get too close to the earth and risk being smashed into the ground by the hurricane-force gales.

At times it seemed as if the hand of a behemoth senselessly hurled the helicopter into the unknown at the speed of light. At other times, the craft seemed to stand still in the eye of a white-whipped tornado, frozen for all eternity.

When the break came, Carter almost missed it.

Exhausted, eyes behind reflecting glasses feeling the sharp pain that preceded snowblindness, the splash of blue sky whisked past.

Carter looked up.

There was a lull in the blizzard. A natural hesitation where the winds and snow parted and the sky and land showed separate and distinct.

He turned the sluggish helicopter.

Yes, blue sky above and the white ground clearly evident below. Without waiting, without looking for landmarks, without even thinking, Carter let his reflexes take over.

He pulled back on the throttle and flipped switches.

Like an exhausted bird, the helicopter settled downward.

Windy snowdevils making little cyclones nearby disappeared in puffs as the blades of the chopper sent new wind back into them.

The helicopter's runners settled onto the ice. Snow skidded away.

He had landed the helicopter in a tunnel of white walls and white ground. And above, the blue sky was fading as once again the blizzard closed in.

Suddenly the wind howled. The helicopter rocked with its blows. The blizzard resumed in all its fury.

He was hopelessly sealed in a tomb of white.

He turned off the motor. Now at last his hands were free enough to call Hawk. He'd expected the helicopter's radio to be out, but not the special AXE radio that worked from anywhere on the globe.

Anywhere but Antarctica in a blizzard. He got nothing but static from the small powerful machine.

Uneasily he checked through his snow survival gear. Everything was there. He pulled on specially heated thermal clothing. He unpacked the small tent.

The temperature in the helicopter dropped. As he waited for another break in the weather, the air in the helicopter closed around him like an icy fist.

Temperatures below 120 degrees Fahrenheit had been recorded in the Antarctic. He was grateful for the carefully thought-out packing that Hawk and he had done at McMurdo.

When another break in the storm at last came, Carter ran outside and tented the helicopter, pounding the stakes deep into the permafrost. Despite his heated clothing, the bitter cold chilled him to the bones.

He returned inside the tent, zipped and locked it safely closed, got back into the helicopter, and climbed inside a sleeping bag.

He heated soup and forced himself to drink it. He was so tired that his hands shook.

As he put the food supplies aside, the blizzard howled relentlessly outside. The deadly storm could easily last nine days as had the one in which the brave Scott and his two remaining companions had died.

But Carter had better equipment. Enough to last two weeks at least. He told himself this as, exhausted, he drifted into sleep.

Carter awoke to silence. A silence that was eerie in its completeness. There wasn't even a tendril of wind. If a single snowflake fell, it was so quiet that he was sure in that moment he could hear it.

He smiled. The blizzard had ended. It had been a short storm, only six hours. He went outside to inspect. Snow was piled to the top of one side of the tent.

Around it, the powerful, erratic gales had swept the snow from some spots, exposing the icy permafrost, while mounding snow elsewhere.

The sun shone. The sky was robin's egg blue. A few fluffy clouds drifted overhead. It was as if the fury of the past few hours had never existed.

There were mountains close by on Carter's right. He didn't know which mountains. He could easily have been swept along the Queen Maud range, but considering the time he'd been in the air, he could also have been blown to more distant ranges. The Pensacola Mountains, perhaps. The Ellsworth Mountains.

No matter. He scooped and swept snow off the tent. He

took it down, shook it out, and repacked it.

He tried the craft's radio, then the small AXE radio. Neither worked. Probably an atmospheric problem.

He took two red and two green flags from his supplies and left the helicopter. He slogged out lines in the snow at ninety-degree angles to the helicopter. They were like compass lines except he didn't know what direction north was. He created a large cross with the helicopter in the center.

He staked a red flag at each end of one line, and a green flag at each end of the other line. He returned to his pilot's seat in the helicopter and crossed his fingers.

He turned on the motor.

It caught, and he let out a deep breath of relief.

He lifted off, flying along one red-flag line that ran parallel to the mountains. The snow and ice glowed nakedly. No sign of humanity.

He flew some distance, then he turned and flew in the opposite direction, crossing where he'd spent the night and the other red flag. Again covering a fair distance, he saw nothing.

He returned to hover over where he'd landed the helicopter.

This time he turned left, following the line of the green flag away from the mountains. Again the giant white wasteland spread empty and desolate beneath him.

Once more he returned to the center of the flags, worried.

He followed the last green flag directly toward the mountains. His eyes automatically scanned the range for passes.

A sudden gust of wind shot down the shadows of a mountainside, spraying ground snow in all directions.

A bright light flashed below. A reflected light. Something . . . perhaps metal . . . caught the sun's rays and reflected them back.

Carter turned the helicopter, taking it slowly along where the wind had swept. He saw the light again.

He found a landing place in the mountain's shadow. Once safely on the ground, he turned off the chopper and put on a backpack filled with special AXE short-term snow supplies. He left the helicopter and walked along the mountain's curve back toward the light.

He hadn't gone far when he heard the blades of another helicopter.

The hairs on the back of his neck stood. He had a sudden sense of danger, an instinct that had saved his life more times than he cared to remember.

He ran back to the helicopter and dragged the small craft over the ice and snow, deep into the mountain's shadow where it was less likely to be noticed.

The other helicopter passed not far away, flying a seemingly straight line over the mountains.

It was a Russian helicopter, apparently making a businesslike trip from one destination to another. The Soviets maintained seven permanent and several seasonal stations in Antarctica.

Which one was Carter close to?

The AXE agent left the helicopter to retrace his steps back to the glimmer of light he'd spotted.

He slogged around white-covered boulders. The chill summer air numbed his face. Ice crunched beneath his feet. He walked down long narrow valleys of snow and ice, having only his sense of direction to rely on.

As he rounded a bend, he saw it.

Rocky Diamond's small jet.

It lay in perfect condition, one wing pointing toward the mountains.

Snow dusted the silvery aircraft. The jet's landing trail extended behind it, some of it still visible thanks to the blizzard's erratic winds. It was a straight landing course, uneventful.

Carter pulled open the door and sniffed the air for the stench of death. Again, nothing.

The jet's interior was perfect . . . and empty of human inhabitants.

Diamond's supplies were all there. Snow survival equipment, clothes, maps, even a bottle of Pernod. But no maverick pilot. And no clues in the papers and maps in the cockpit.

Carter went outside. Apparently Diamond had simply disappeared.

The AXE agent didn't believe that.

He trudged around the jet in slowly widening circles. Perhaps the blizzard had left another trail or clue.

He found the skimobile tracks in another mountain shadow. From their direction, they had come and gone from the jet.

He walked beside them, studying them. One of the two sets of tracks was deeper, as if carrying a heavier load. Maybe carrying an unconscious Rocky Diamond away.

Carter reached into the insulated pocket of his backpack and took out the small but powerful AXE radio. Perhaps whatever was disturbing the atmosphere had eased.

He got through to Hawk on the first try.

"Where the devil have you been, N3?"

"Damned if I know."

Carter described the storm that must have disrupted radio contact, and the "night" he'd spent in the helicopter with the blizzard howling outside. Then he told Hawk about Rocky Diamond's jet.

"Interesting," Hawk said, but Carter could hear the edge of excitement in his voice. "Hold on while I take a fix on you."

The butane lighter snapped into life back in McMurdo as Hawk worked. Soon the AXE director exhaled noisily.

"Damn! He's almost on top of Novolazarevskaya!" It was another voice. Colonel Chester ffolkes. "Blenkochev'll be breathing down his neck!"

"N3?" Hawk said in the distance. "Did you hear?"

"Yes, sir. Princess Astrid Coast must be over the mountains," he said. "Colonel ffolkes, any word about Mike?"

"Giving them all a bad time at the hospital. Be out soon, bless her," Colonel ffolkes said, his voice relieved. "Jolly

good work, Carter. Novolazarevskaya! It's critical we re-
solve this problem soon.''

"You've learned something new?" Carter asked.

He stamped his feet and rubbed his nose with a mittened
hand. He would be warmer standing in the sunshine, but now
he was concerned about being seen. Shadows were safer.

"Unfortunately," Hawk said. "There's been a second
case of the disease that killed the Soviet attaché. Colonel
ffolkes sent the doctor who treated the attaché to investigate.
A Chilean soldier who was in that country's Antarctic base at
Bernardo O'Higgins. This one didn't have the Silver Dove
tattoo. The man's dead.''

"It reminds me of the deaths in Europe after World War
Two," ffolkes said to Hawk. "Remember? Patients dying in
hospital for no apparent reason."

"No one could forget," Hawk said grimly. "Penicillin so
diluted that it was worse than worthless. Doctors relied on it,
a miracle drug, and they didn't bother to treat with anything
else.''

"It took us a long time to find the bloody sources. The
murderers.''

"Never did get them all. Finally our U.S. labs solved the
problem by producing so much penicillin that the black
market demand for it stopped.''

"Blenkochev?" Carter said.

"It was rumored that he ran a big black market penicillin
business," ffolkes said. "The profits lined his pocket and the
Kremlin's depleted war treasury.''

"But we couldn't find any conclusive proof," Hawk said.

"Except that he had money, David. And black market
connections that were astounding. If anyone needed real
penicillin, they could get it through him.''

"Remember the beer garden on Konigsallee?" Hawk said
to his old friend. "Blenkochev on the tables?"

The two agency heads laughed heartily. It was a joke at
Blenkochev's expense that would be treasured until the last
witness died. In the short-lived, dangerous business they

were in, laughter was a rare commodity. The healthiest members of the community took advantage of it whenever possible.

"So," ffolkes said at last, a smile still in his voice.

"Yes, so," Hawk agreed, puffing cheerfully far away.

From the sound of Hawk's voice, Carter knew the AXE director had once again made peace with his job. There was excitement to be found in sitting behind a desk and planning, an excitement different from the adventures of the field. Still, it was excitement.

"Get on with it, N3," Hawk continued. "Follow the skimobile tracks. Find Diamond if possible. Find out what's going on at the Soviet base at Novolazarevskaya."

"And watch out for that rotter Blenkochev," ffolkes added. "He was once the best and most ruthless killer in the world. Only better than Hawk in the sense that he was so heartless."

There was silence. The two men had nothing more to add, each lost in memories of the past. Carter signed off, put the radio back in his pack, and hiked back to the helicopter for snow-camping supplies. It would take several days to cross the mountains. He wanted to be prepared.

THIRTEEN

Nick Carter smoothly slid one ski ahead of the other. It continued to be a beautiful Antarctic day, clear and bright. He followed the skimobile tracks up a gentle snowy grade using cross-country Trek skis, flexible and long, and ski poles for his mittened hands. On his back he carried a backpack and sleeping bag.

In the sunlight, the snow was dazzling. Millions of little light particles glimmered like diamonds. The skimobile tracks were alternately visible and snow-covered. He followed them over the sparkling white carpet in the easy rhythm of the cross-country skier. It was a form of long-stride, slip-slide jogging that stretched the muscles until they sang.

Two wandering albatrosses flew overhead, a sign that the coast was just across the mountains. They were big birds, with eleven-foot wingspans that they rode like magic carpets as they circumnavigated the southern half of the world. Occasionally the two glanced at one another, like humans aware of their loved ones. Wandering albatrosses usually mated for life, and for them that could be more than fifty years.

Carter considered this as he pushed ahead into the isolation of the mountains. Sunlight filtered through a nearby glacier, producing an ethereal blue haze. Many of life's lessons could be learned in this beautiful desolation. Love, loyalty, courage.

Occasional thundering crashes sounded in the distance. It was mountainsides of snow too heavy to cling any longer, or the ends of glaciers sheering off in relief. This was a dramatic land, and not safe.

As he skied along, small mounds of snow slid down crevices and plopped at his feet. He passed through narrow valleys, over ridges, between boulders, always climbing as he followed the tracks. Snow and ice hung to sheer walls on either side of him. Suspended. Waiting to crash down and fill the valley he crossed. Waiting to smother him in soft wet oblivion.

Alone in the splendid solitude, the sky and sun his only companions, he skied on, occasionally scooping up a handful of snow and letting it melt in his mouth. It was fresh and clean, untainted by salty streets and smog. No wonder people were drawn here. If he weren't on assignment, it could almost be his interrupted vacation.

He stroked his soft beard and looked ahead. The skimobile tracks continued upward, always climbing.

Then he heard the jet.

He skied swiftly into a shadow.

The jet swooped low over the mountains. Carter saw the markings. Soviet markings. The craft made three passes, then soared off toward Molodezhnaya, the Soviet Antarctic headquarters.

Carter resumed his journey, sobered by concern that he'd been discovered.

He had to go on. He had no choice. He concentrated on the task at hand. Soon he was once more caught in the hypnotic rhythm of the cross-country skier. He would continue one more hour, then make camp and rest.

Carter herringboned up a steep snowy slope, his long skis cutting crosshatched steps as he followed the more agile skimobile. Probably a Russian skimobile. Maybe a Silver Dove skimobile. Carrying a helpless American. Diamond.

Antarctica was a preserve for wildlife, but not yet a preserve for humanity.

Then Carter smiled. Antarctica's spirit of universal peace and harmony was sufficiently strong that all of the continent's stations were open by treaty agreement to visitors from any nation at any time. He wondered about Novolazarevskaya. The Russian station.

He wasn't about to ski right up to it and ask whether their open-door policy applied to spies. Not with Blenkochev so close.

Sweating, he reached the top of the crest. Accordian pleats of snowy valleys and rocky mountaintops spread before him. He wiped a mitten across his face. His breath was silver steam in the air.

He scanned the majestic and deserted Antarctic mountains. On the other side of them was Novolazarevskaya. Exactly why had Blenkochev left Russia? What did he hope to accomplish in New Zealand?

A new answer to the question was beginning to form in Carter's mind.

Then he heard an intrusion in the white silence.

The helicopter came quietly, its rotors muffled behind a mountainside.

There were no shadows on the crest where Carter stood. Nowhere for him to hide.

On his skis, Carter plunged back down the slope he'd just climbed. Pain shot through his tired body as he slid and fell.

He dropped deep into the shadow of the ravine.

The helicopter was moving slowly. A Russian helicopter. Obviously looking for someone . . . or something.

Carter stayed in the darkest part of the shadow, his muscles and bones aching. The observers in the helicopter might spot his ski trail, but they shouldn't be able to see him.

He watched.

The helicopter approached. A head was peering out over the side.

Without pausing, the helicopter slowly moved past.

Carter breathed deeply, waiting.

The helicopter moved on, doing thoroughly once what the Soviet jet had done quickly three times.

Carter allowed himself a small smile of triumph, then he tested his body for bruises and broken bones. He was intact, but very tired. He would make camp as soon as he could find a good sheltered spot.

Once more he slogged up the slope, his remarkable stamina and strength surging new power back into his exhausted body.

At the top again where the mountains spread around him in a rocky panorama, he skied on, dipping in and out of canyons, following the skimobile's trail.

Time passed, the Antarctic sun making little progress. Carter watched for a good campsite.

At last he rounded a bend in layered shadows where boulders and snowslides covered a flat apron of land.

The snow gave a good level spot, not large, but large enough. The boulders offered good shelter. Some as large as rooms, they'd spilled one on top of the other until a roof formed over part of the flat area.

Carter dropped his backpack beneath the roof.

He'd pitch the tent here, a shelter against another storm. He'd be protected from helicopter surveillance by the boulders above.

Then he saw the shadow move.

Amid the sounds of dropping snow and distant avalanches, he heard the slick noise of a ski sliding.

It was across from him, someone entering the flat area from the other side.

Quickly he pulled on his backpack, took off his mitten, and flipped his stiletto into his hand. In Antarctica, only a madman shot a gun. The noise would cause avalanches and destruction for miles around.

He skied swiftly back out the way he'd come. He was careful to stay in the same tracks.

When he was out of sight of the flat area, he looked over

his shoulder and saw his single ski trail. He heard the sounds of the other skier, heard the pause as the skier discovered Carter's trail, then the rapidity of strokes as he pursued Carter.

Carter swung his arms and leaped off the trail, landing on his back in the soft snow.

With his mitten and arm he brushed the snowbank smooth again as he backed off behind an enormous boulder.

With luck, the pursuer would see only the ski trail continuing on with the skimobile tracks.

Carter skied quietly around the boulder to where he could watch the newcomer's pursuit.

The slip-slide of the oncoming skis were muffled sounds in the Antarctic stillness, the noises absorbed by the vast snow.

First Carter saw the peaked blue fiberfill hat that was fastened beneath the chin, then the thick blue parka and trousers. The skis were Russian.

The man was small, agile, his face bent low as he studied Carter's trail.

As he came in sight of the place where Carter had jumped off, he slowed. He raised his face to scan ahead.

Carter smiled.

It was Blenkochev's comrade, the man with the yellow Mazda.

The expression on the small-featured face was one of puzzlement. Something wasn't right, the expression said, but he wasn't sure exactly what. He skied ahead slowly.

Swiftly Carter returned around the boulder to follow.

The knife glinted in the sun.

The assistant's knife was waiting for Carter where he'd jumped off the trail. It was now Blenkochev's pal's turn to smile. He'd figured out Carter's trick in leaving the trail. He'd doubled back to meet him.

"You shouldn't be here," the Russian agent said softly, the knife pointed at Carter's chin. He spoke in English.

"Why not?" Carter answered in Russian, showing his stiletto.

The stiletto was a diversion.

He threw the other hand up and knocked the Russian's knife flying.

The Russian's toe clips were already released. His boots free, he kicked.

"Because this is none of your business!" he said.

Carter ducked.

The Russian changed targets. His foot unerringly caught the stiletto in Carter's hand, sending Hugo flying overhead.

Quickly Carter unsnapped his skis from his feet.

The knife and stiletto were nowhere in sight.

The two agents thrashed through the snow. Circled. Their boots sank six inches into the soft powder.

Again the Russian's foot lashed out.

Carter caught it.

The Russian twisted.

Carter yanked.

Caught by the snow, the two fell forward.

Wrestled.

Suddenly Carter veered back, his eyes wide.

Breasts. The Russian had breasts. A woman. Why the walk was different. Why the tam-o'-shanter was pulled low to the ears.

The woman swung a fist.

Carter spun to the side.

He reached back, unsnapped the chin strap, and whipped up the woman's blue peaked cap.

Long flaxen hair cascaded to the shoulders of the blue parka. The hair was like strands of silk, flying free in the icy Antarctic air. The small-featured face came into perspective. A too-small man turned into a beautifully proportioned woman with full lips, straight nose, and wide eyes bright under the cold sun. She was the blonde in the airport photograph Mike had showed him. The beautiful blonde.

"I'll be damned," Carter murmured.

"Took you long enough," she said, slugging him in the chin. "It works every time."

Taken by surprise, reeling from the blow, Carter slugged back.

She went limp.

He caught her before she hit the ground. He hadn't intended to knock her out.

She was light. Her head fell back, the pale blond hair drifting long to the snow.

He laid her down, then found the knife and the stiletto buried in nearby snowbanks. He put on his skis and picked her up. She moaned, still unconscious. He threw her over his shoulder in a fireman's carry, grabbed her skis with his other hand, and skied back to the flat place to make camp.

He was heating soup when she awoke. Four handfuls of snow and a package of dehydrated meat, beans, and vegetable soup mix in a lightweight pot.

"How much longer?" she inquired as she rubbed her chin. "I could eat an elephant."

"Don't you want to fight first?"

"Later. When I have my strength back."

She was gutsy as well as beautiful.

The soup smelled delicious cooking over the solid-fuel pellet. Carter had pitched the one-man tent, scraped and rewaxed both their skis, thrown their sleeping mats and bags into the tent, and searched her backpack. He'd found her Walther in a side pocket and a radio in the other. He'd put both with her knife into his backpack. The rest of her gear was standard for snow camping.

"It's nice to see you don't hold a grudge," he said.

She smiled radiantly and took the cup of hot soup he handed her.

"In Russia we have a saying, Never bite the hand that feeds you."

"Interesting how proverbs cross all lines."

"The universality of human nature," she said and shrugged.

They ate.

"Leaving Novolazarevskaya?" he said.

"Maybe."

"Your direction wasn't toward it. But maybe it was toward something else?"

"If you have something to say, speak plainly."

"All right," he said slowly. "What kind of secret work is going on down here that's killing people with diseases your scientists can't control and our scientists don't recognize?"

"Perhaps you're asking the wrong person," the deep, cultured Russian voice said.

Carter looked up.

Leon Blenkochev, the ruthless head of the KGB's powerful K-GOL agency, stood at the edge of the overhanging boulders. He was pointing a Luger at Carter's heart.

FOURTEEN

Nick Carter hadn't heard a sound, not a sliding ski, not a cough. He looked with respect at Leon Blenkochev.

"The helicopter and jet spotted me?" he said.

The KGB czar waved the question off.

"Throw your gun and knife over here," he said imperiously.

He waited until Carter had tossed the weapons ten feet to his boots, then the K-GOL director skied forward.

His lumpy Slavic face glowed in the sunshine. He wore a blue fiberfill suit like the woman's, a pointed cap, reflecting sunglasses, a backpack, and perfume. The perfume was fragrant. Not too much. The affectation of a man who was powerful enough to not give a damn.

Blenkochev was stout and strong, in his late sixties. Much more than merely active, he exuded a sense of vigorous self-possession and destiny that would attract attention wherever he went.

Here, in Antarctica, with a gun pointed unwaveringly at Carter as he skied easily toward the AXE agent, he certainly had Carter's attention. Blenkochev didn't bluff. He didn't have to.

"At last I meet the great Blenkochev," Carter said and smiled.

"Don't be cute, N3," Blenkochev said. "It doesn't become you."

"You recognize me."

"Notoriety always gets my attention."

"I'm impressed, considering that the KGB's filing system is a hall full of cardboard boxes."

Blenkochev scowled, and his blond comrade quickly hid a smile behind her cup of soup. She was good-natured, too.

"I'm hollow, Anna," Blenkochev announced.

He stared pointedly at the soup pot. He'd deal with Carter later. He handed his gun to the agent Anna, and she leveled it at Carter.

"Did you bring food?" Carter asked. "This is not the Antarctic Salvation Army."

Blenkochev took off his backpack and dropped it into the snow. He untied an insulated sitting mat.

"No?" he said. "Perhaps it's a version of the 1980 Olympics. You don't want to play? You go home. Hurray U.S.A."

Carter laughed.

"You want a medal for that?" Blenkochev asked and chuckled. "You didn't get any in 1980."

Blenkochev sat on the mat on the snow, and perfume wafted into the air. He extended his legs stiffly in front of him. For a moment a look of pleasure came onto his face, pleasure in where he was, in what he was doing. Then he quickly erased it. He was in control.

"First we eat. Then we talk," the KGB czar said. "Anna, there are supplies in my pack. I'll take my weapon now."

She handed the gun to him, then unzipped his pack. Her flaxen hair flowed over the deep blue of her padded suit. She had a sultry face made even more attractive by intelligence. A dangerous combination for an enemy. A valuable one for a friend. Once more the gun was aimed at Carter.

"Now I know why you weren't concerned when you woke

up," Carter told her as she prepared more soup. "You expected Blenkochev."

"It was a possibility," she said.

"Are there more of you?"

"How many do you want?" Blenkochev said. "All this concern for quantity. A pity. It's made quality a thing of the past."

"I suspect the past wasn't all that different from today," Carter said mildly. "Hindsight isn't twenty-twenty."

"And the present isn't all that pretty," Blenkochev said. He crossed his arms, resting the gun on the left, still pointing it at Carter. "When the present is unpleasant and the future worrisome, we tend to retreat into the familiarity of the past."

"And what are you worried about?" Carter asked.

"Quality, obviously," Blenkochev said. A small smile curved at the corners of his mouth as he played with Carter's words. "I'd prefer a fine paella or a hearty bouillabaisse. Instead I get freeze-dried predigested soup that's been rejected by the gourmet palates of our Siberian miners and your television addicts. That makes it good enough for the KGB. But I'm not complaining."

Anna handed a full cup of soup to Blenkochev, and he sipped. His hand shook slightly. Being in the field wasn't as easy for him as it once was, but his ruddy face and eagerness showed that he was enjoying it thoroughly.

"I hear you're a killer," Carter said.

"It's been said," Blenkochev replied over the steaming soup. It would take more than accusations to shock him out of his equilibrium. "That makes two of us, Killmaster."

Within three minutes in the Antarctic air the soup would be cold. Now the old agent drank rapidly.

"Why are you here?" Anna asked Carter while her superior finished his meal.

"It started as a vacation," Carter said, "but no one would believe me."

"Michelle Strange, otherwise known as Mike," Anna

said. "I believe you had a sexual interlude with her at a remote mountain jail. Don't you consider that kinky? It is the right word . . . kinky?"

"It's what you had in mind," Carter said. "Were you there too?"

"I'm not Silver Dove, if that's what you mean." A note of indignation slipped into her voice.

"Killmaster," Blenkochev interrupted, "I require a tent. I have an adequate one strapped to the bottom of my pack. If you would be so kind . . . "

Blenkochev undid the straps and kicked it across the snow to Carter. It was an order, not a request. He casually rubbed the side of his gun against his cheek, then handed his empty cup to Anna. She refilled it.

"Shall I get out your toothbrush too?" Carter smiled.

"Thank you, no. I have it in my pocket."

"Clean socks? Undershorts? A battery-run shaver?"

"Unfortunately, there wasn't room to pack them. The next time I decide to go into the field I'll choose my assignment more carefully."

Blenkochev pushed his pack behind his back and leaned back comfortably while Carter went to work.

"Perhaps you'd like to hear an AXE bedtime story?" Carter asked as he unrolled Blenkochev's light one-man tent.

"I have no objection," Blenkochev said. There was just a hint of suspicion in his voice. Again he drank soup.

"The helicopter and jet weren't looking for me," Carter said. "They were looking for you. And you're here alone. No support."

He spread the tent at the other end of the roofed-over flat area and got out stakes. He looked at Blenkochev.

As if unconcerned, the K-GOL chief shrugged.

"At one time Silver Dove must have been one of your most trusted assassination arms," Carter went on. "You recruit from athletes for their physical vigor, from university students for their intellects, and from embassy staffs for their contacts . . . why not from bigots for the power of their hatreds? A man who hates enough will do anything to keep his hatred intact. It's what he lives for. But then something happened. Silver Dove got out of hand. Little by little. Hardly noticeable. Until now you have a full-fledged crisis on your hands. And it is *your* crisis. The Politburo won't just take your *dacha* away if Silver Dove accomplishes what it threatens.''

''And what does it threaten, my fine young Turk?''

Blenkochev tossed his empty cup to Anna. She caught it with one mittened hand, then pushed it in and out of the snow to wash it. Blenkochev knew that Carter didn't know the threat, and his smile mocked the other deductions Carter had made.

''Whatever it was, it was big and important enough to force the biggest target in Russia out of the safety of the motherland. Burnout or midlife crisis or even longing for the past didn't bring you into the field. Although I think you're glad to be here,'' Carter added. He pounded tent stakes. ''It's fear. Plain, old-fashioned fear.''

He looked over his shoulder and saw Blenkochev bristle. The gun weaved ever so slightly. Still, if Carter were to accomplish his mission, he had to go on. Blenkochev had to be shocked into changing his attitude just enough to help him.

''Not only fear of losing your job and maybe your life,'' Carter continued, ''but also fear for the safety of large numbers of people. Maybe even for the world. Your world in particular, and mine by circumstance. So you came to New Zealand with Anna. Only one assistant. Your one concession to age. But a woman so you'd attract less attention. You investigated at the embassy, and she went into the field. Disguised. She heard about our missing flyer and was on her way to look up Mackenzie when by accident she drove past Mike and me after the crash. She recognized me and left the first aid supplies. Already she'd begun to help me. Why?''

Apparently disinterested, the dishes done and repacked, Anna lay back on her pack and lit a cigarette. A calm professional. She blew rings into the cold air.

"Because we weren't fighting," Carter said and popped up light aluminum poles, the tent's skeleton. "Because we were after the same thing, and if she kept tabs on me and I found it first, she could steal it. The only issue was what."

"And you don't know," Blenkochev said, satisfied.

"I can make a close guess. It has to do with biological warfare."

Blenkochev said nothing, pursing his lips. His silence told Carter he was right.

"A new strain of bacteria or virus that's being developed by Silver Dove somewhere down here. Maybe at Novolazarevskaya, although I doubt it because Antarctic stations have to remain open to everyone. But nearby, probably. Near enough so that Diamond—when he had to make an emergency landing—saw something he shouldn't have, and had to be carted away. It puts you in an awkward position. With biological warfare, you can't just rush a place. Someone could break one little vial, and the world is contaminated. If you're dealing with fanatics, an order they find disagreeable will be disobeyed. And people whose main motivation is hatred don't respond to reasoning. So if you can't use force, orders, or reasoning, you have to outmaneuver, outwit, and outflank them."

Carter slipped the skeleton poles inside the tent.

"Go on," Blenkochev said. "I'm listening."

"Which also explains why you didn't kill me"—Carter smiled—"and why you're holding that ridiculous gun on me. You won't fire it out here. You'd bring the whole damned mountainside down on us. That'll never get you reinstated with Chernenko."

Now it was Blenkochev's turn to smile, and he held up the other hand. In it was a stiletto, the twin of Carter's own.

"I'm not completely unprepared," the wily old agent murmured.

"No, and you've let me ramble like this for a purpose. You want to know how much Hawk knows. How much I've guessed. And whether you want me to help. Much better to have me with you than bumbling around maybe making matters worse. The other option, of course, is to kill me.''

A deep throaty laugh rumbled from Blenkochev. Anna watched Carter with respect.

''Ah, N3, too bad you can't be bought!'' He held his belly and laughed. ''I would love to steal you from Hawk. Finally I would get even with the old bastard!''

As the mighty KGB man roared with laughter, Carter snapped the tent skeleton in place, then sat back on his haunches to admire his work.

''Your tent's finished,'' he said mildly. ''Now I'd like to hear your proposal.''

''Give Anna back her weapons first,'' Blenkochev said. He took off his glasses and wiped a sleeve across his eyes. ''I know you've got them hidden somewhere.''

''And my Luger?''

''Anna,'' Blenkochev said.

The old agent was tired, and at last comfortable. He wasn't going to move until he had to.

Anna fetched Carter's gun while he took from his backpack the Walther and knife. They exchanged weapons, and Anna gave him a smile of curiosity.

''Did you hear about the Chilean soldier?'' Carter asked as he settled back onto his own insulated snow mat.

''Unfortunately, yes,'' Blenkochev said. ''Another nail in the coffin. A group from Chile visited the Novolazarevskaya area last week. There was no way to keep tabs on all of them, and besides it doesn't look friendly if it's too obvious that they're being watched. One or more must have slipped away. Either they knew what they were doing, or they didn't.'' The KGB man shrugged. ''It's immaterial now. Now that the one's dead.''

''If there were survivors, then you must know where they were here.''

Blenkochev allowed himself a short smile.

"I have certain information," he admitted.

"Don't bother being modest, Blenkochev. No one believes it."

Again the belly laugh.

"No wonder you're Hawk's favorite," he chuckled.

"So we're going to find this secret installation," Carter said. "The installation that your New Zealand attaché also visited without anyone's knowledge."

"The same," Blenkochev agreed. He stood up and stretched. "Now I must sleep. I'm old, but I don't admit it in Moscow. Here I don't give a damn. Here my age can be a hindrance." He checked his watch, his face turning grim. "We leave in four hours. No longer. Rest. I expect you both in top form." He stared north across the mountains as if he could see into the future. "This insanity could destroy my country."

Dignified and powerful as an old, seasoned lion, Blenkochev stalked into his tent and dropped the flap. The perfume lingered for a moment, then was swept away in a light breeze.

Carter and Anna were silent, deep in their own worry.

"You're standing guard?" Carter said at last, noting Anna's lack of interest in pitching her own tent.

"Sitting guard," she said, relaxed back against her pack.

Her blond hair glowed like gold in the sunshine. Her face was solemn, watchful, its attention directed at Carter. As soon as he retired to his tent, she would focus her alertness on the area around them.

She laid the Walther on her chest and held the knife loosely in her hand. Beautiful, intelligent, good-natured, and a thorough professional. Good reasons for Blenkochev to have chosen her, but there had to be more. A reason why he trusted her more than any of his other agents. Not only was his career and life-style on the line, but also the world he'd helped to shape for the last forty years. He had less compassion for the world than he had pride in the immortality of his work.

"You grew up in Moscow?" Carter asked.

"Yes."

She was waiting for him to leave, wanted to be at her job. Like many agents, she worked better alone. Yet she was interested in him. Couldn't take her eyes off him. One more reason why she wanted him to leave.

"I appreciate your help back in New Zealand," he said and stood. He didn't want to leave, but it was necessary that he, too, keep his distance.

She smiled up at him.

"I was a music student," she said. "Violin. Chamber music. Does that help?"

"Not really. Why did Blenkochev choose you?"

She looked at him, her face now expressionless. She was trying to decide whether to tell him anything and, if she did, whether to tell him the truth. She was a woman worth knowing. At last she cleared her throat.

"He's my father."

The one answer Carter hadn't guessed. She watched him quizzically to see how he'd take the news. It was hard to imagine Blenkochev sexually involved with anyone. But even the most outrageous, the most cold-blooded, the most extensively distracted sometimes committed the grace of physical intimacy. Her mother must have been remarkable. He hoped that Blenkochev had loved her.

"He's a lucky man," Carter said and went into his tent.

FIFTEEN

Nick Carter, Leon Blenkochev, and Anna Blenkochev skied across the skimobile tracks into untouched snow. Blenkochev was leading. He knew where he was going and didn't want to lose any element of surprise he might acquire from arriving at the Silver Dove installation in an unexpected way.

Occasionally he used a sun compass from his backpack to take a reading. Knowing local Antarctic time and that the summer sun circles the horizon at about fifteen degrees an hour, he figured with close accuracy where they were and where they needed to go next.

That hadn't been necessary to find Carter. Blenkochev and Anna had crossed the skimobile tracks first, not knowing Carter was in the area. The KGB leader had sent his daughter to investigate in one direction while he'd gone the other. When she hadn't returned as scheduled, he'd come after her and discovered Carter as well.

Now the three skied through the pristine snow, taking turns breaking trail. Carter found himself watching Anna, intrigued by something he couldn't name. Occasionally he caught her watching him.

A few sooty albatrosses passed overhead, riding the air currents. They were perfect gliding machines. The stronger the wind, the more effortless seemed their flight. The sky remained its spectacular clear blue, the bright sun giving little warmth to the sparkling land.

At last, still very high in the mountains, wind whipping around them, Blenkochev signaled to slow.

Leading, he pushed quietly ahead. His body was hunched with concentration. He must have been exhausted, but he gave no sign of it. He headed into the gale.

He stopped at a large sheer rock face that was blown free of snow. He unsnapped his skis and plodded forward, sinking with each step.

He motioned for Carter and Anna to follow.

He disappeared around the rock face as the two agents skied forward, unsnapped their skis, and followed.

Below them extended a valley. It was deep and long, ridged by boulders and rocks naked to the sun. It was an area of almost constant wind that kept any projecting objects free of snow.

Surrounded by peaks and hanging rocks, it would be a difficult valley to see from the air. A hidden valley.

There appeared to be movement on the valley's long, narrow snow-white floor. Carter couldn't quite make out what it was. He stroked his beard and studied the valley.

Blenkochev handed tiny, powerful binoculars to Carter.

"Over there," Blenkochev said, gesturing.

Two sliding doors so big that they'd be oversize even for an airplane hangar were fitted into the granite at the side of the valley. They were painted a dull gray to match the rock. They were ajar. Workmen outfitted in stark white insulated snowsuits passed in and out, some driving white jeeps, others on white skis. The workers were almost invisible.

"Silver Dove?"

"Looks like Silver Dove now," Blenkochev said curtly. "A regular Soviet base before. We abandoned it when we signed the Antarctic Treaty. There was no longer a fight for the continent. It's been so long now that it's mostly forgotten."

"Silver Dove didn't forget," Anna murmured. She looked at Carter and smiled.

Blenkochev glanced at his daughter, his assistant, his employee. Pride briefly filled his broad Slavic face. Then he banished it. No room for sentiment when there was a job to be done. He asked no quarter, and gave none. Not even to his daughter.

"We're going to stand out like sore thumbs down there," Carter said, gesturing at the Blenkochevs' blue clothes and at his own khaki.

"In the end, it may save us," Blenkochev said quietly.

He dropped his backpack and squatted to unzip it. He pulled out a gunny sack and opened it.

"Here's that emergency gear you brought," he said loudly to Carter. "We'll bury it. Pick it up later in case of emergency."

He opened the insulated sack and showed Carter a small radio similar to Carter's, emergency rations, a lightweight snow blanket that folded to the size of a handkerchief, and first aid gear. He'd come prepared.

"I'll take that!"

The voice was sharp, commanding. From above.

"Throw it up!"

The lookout pointed a long-barreled rifle down at them. It was a special air gun, silent. Perfectly safe in the avalanche-prone wasteland.

The lookout in his white deep-freeze clothes stood on a rock mesa. He could have been there for hours, could have watched their approach, hidden, waiting while he radioed ahead for instructions.

"Excellent," Blenkochev said.

Suddenly more men swarmed around either side of the sheer rock face, all dressed in white like German ski soldiers of World War II. They were stealthy, drifting forward like part of the landscape. Each had a small silver dove embroidered on the material over his heart.

Blenkochev raised a hand full of command.

"I am Blenkochev," he said majestically in his cultured Russian. "I've caught the notorious Nick Carter. He's the imperialist AXE agent from that overweight pig the United States."

His steely eyes swept the all-male Soviet faces, demanding that they listen and obey. Their guerrilla lessons hadn't included a chapter on a man such as Blenkochev. They were off balance. Instantly he saw this. For the moment, they were malleable. He smiled coldly at the quiet men and continued.

"He's a dangerous American spy-whore," he said. "I've brought him a long way, and we're tired."

He gestured with disdain at Carter and nodded at Anna. She took her clue and reached into Carter's backpack for his weapons.

"Who's in charge here?" the powerful Blenkochev said.

"I am, sir," replied one of the men.

He stepped forward, his air rifle pointed at Carter. Only his tanned face glowing against the brilliant snow showed the possibility of something human under all that white padding.

Anna tucked Carter's weapons under her arms. Disapproving, the Silver Dove glanced at the female agent. Women belonged at home with a house full of babies, not in rugged Antarctica pretending they had the stamina and intelligence of a man.

"My daughter," Blenkochev said curtly, "and my assistant."

"Yes, sir," the Silver Dove said, impressed by the blood relationship but not by the work relationship. "I'll take those, comrade."

He collected the weapons and allowed himself a discreet leer that he thought Blenkochev couldn't see. If she weren't good enough for a man to marry, the daughter had possibilities as something else. Bigotry found excuses for whatever a perverse man could imagine.

"You'll take us down," Blenkochev announced. "Now."

He, too, looked at Anna, but his expression was one of warning. He was telling her not to kill the chauvinistic oaf. At least not yet.

She nodded grimly, and Carter, the Blenkochevs, and the party of Silver Doves skied around the boulder and down a long, winding trail into the valley.

The massive entrance area inside the Silver Dove facility was icy cold. The bitter wind whistled through the open steel doors and over the trucks, jeeps, skimobiles, and small helicopters that were parked in tidy rows. Other vehicles came and went. Exhaust swirled and stank in the air.

Their skis over their shoulders, the three agents and their escort group passed among the vehicles. Some were painted stark white with faint silver doves drawn on the fenders. Others were olive drab with Russian markings. None of the helicopters looked like the one that had been searching the mountains.

The group continued toward the back of the warehouse where doors were cut into more granite.

Workmen in insulated white suits checked wheels and gas, carried clipboards stacked with papers, and spoke into walkie-talkies. Small silver doves were embroidered over their hearts. They were all white and male.

They looked with little interest at the newcomers, then returned to their work. Either those who worked at the hidden Silver Dove facility were used to visitors, or their natural curiosity had been trained out of them.

Carter watched Blenkochev.

The Russian's face was impassive, but the eyes were watchful. They scanned the enormous room. He was looking for something. Or someone. Briefly his eyes settled on a square man with a bushy black mustache. If there was recognition from either, they hid it well. Carter would watch for the reappearance of the square man with the bushy black mustache.

●   ●   ●

The man beside the wide walnut desk was also dressed in white—a white silk three-piece tropical business suit, nipped in at the waist.

He stood beside the desk as Carter, Blenkochev, and Anna filed into the office, now accompanied by only three of their original escorts. The three Silver Doves kept their air rifles pointed at Carter. In the corner, a heater hissed with warm air.

"Blenkochev," the man beside the desk said in a contained voice.

Blenkochev nodded affirmation.

"I should have known it'd be you, Skobelev," he said. "It's good to see you."

From General Yevgeny Skobelev's breast pocket flowed a brilliant red silk handkerchief. The small dove on the pocket was embroidered with shining silver thread. His shoes were white, too, and polished until they reflected the walnut desk. His shirt was pale pink, only slightly more rosy than his skin. With his thick white hair, light blue eyes, and baby-pink complexion he was a portrait in pastels. Except for the bright red handkerchief . . . which framed the silver dove with bloody importance.

"Why are you here, Blenkochev?" General Skobelev said.

The Soviet general was giving nothing away, not even a gracious greeting. He walked behind his desk and sat in a leather-covered chair.

He had all the amenities, even paintings of Russian landscapes on his four plastered office walls, lamps instead of overhead fluorescent lights, and an apartment-size refrigerator on the floor behind his chair. Beside it was a second door, this one with a peephole.

Blenkochev took it all in with one haughty glance. He wasn't intimidated. He dropped into a leather-covered chair in front of the desk, crossed his legs, took off his mittens, and opened his parka. His perfume filled the room.

When Carter tried to sit, Blenkochev waved a hand, and the three guards backed the AXE agent into a corner.

Carter didn't protest, fulfilling his role. He didn't trust Blenkochev, but he would play along with him for a while. He needed to know exactly what was happening in the Silver Dove installation. What he'd told Blenkochev were only educated guesses, and he needed confirmation. He needed concrete information on which to judge what to do. Concrete information to give Hawk.

Anna watched, then sat, too, and loosened her thick clothing.

"Have any coffee?" Blenkochev asked, smiling disarmingly.

Skobelev looked at him briefly, then at one of the Silver Dove guards. The guard nodded and left the room.

"Now, Leon," General Skobelev said. "What's this all about?"

"I might ask you the same question," Blenkochev said arrogantly, "except that it's my business to know the answer first." He slapped his hands down on the wooden arms of his chair. The sound reverberated in the small room, and the two remaining guards jumped. "I've come to join you, Yevgeny. My daughter and I. No other way to explain it. I brought Carter to show my sincerity."

Skobelev exercised self-control. His mouth dropped only a fraction of an inch. Then he reassembled his face, and his manner was once again that of the polished and mighty Soviet general, close to the Politburo, right-hand man to Chernenko, a face known to all Russia for the many appearances it made in official Soviet news photographs celebrating the First of May and other military occasions.

He studied Blenkochev. The personal power of the two Soviet leaders filled the room.

"My men heard you planning to bury supplies with Carter," Skobelev said. "Emergency supplies that you'd return for. Need later, after taking our base perhaps."

"A ruse," Blenkochev explained smoothly, "a distraction. I wanted to stay in one place long enough for your men to find me."

"Carter had his weapons," the Silver Dove leader shot back. "He was your companion, not your captive."

"Carter is notorious for escaping," Blenkochev said easily. "Sometimes success is more certain with trickery than with force. And remember, he's David Hawk's favorite. Some of his training came from Hawk personally."

The name of the mighty AXE chief gave Skobelev pause. "Yes. David Hawk."

The white-haired Russian general tapped his fingers on the desk top. From his expression, Carter guessed that he'd had his own run-ins with Hawk. The experiences were enough to convince Skobelev that Carter was too dangerous to capture easily, and worth the difficulty of outwitting.

"Do you know our aims?" Skobelev warned the potential convert Blenkochev. "What we plan to do? A man with a queasy stomach and no vision belongs back in the safety of Mother Russia, not here on the frontier of a new way of life."

"I know enough to intrigue me," Blenkochev said and smiled. "Enough to think you're on to something important. A superiority of life forms. As for the rest, perhaps you'd better fill me in."

The door to Skobelev's office opened, and the guard returned with a tray and two mugs of steaming coffee. He put the mugs on the desk, one in front of Skobelev, and the other in front of Blenkochev. None for Anna.

Angry, Anna stared at her father, but the flicker of his eyelashes warned her to be silent. They had a job to do. No time to right petty injustices. She compressed her lips and folded her hands in her lap. Two bright spots flamed on her cheeks. She looked at Carter, and he saw the depth of her sense of injustice. She was a passionate woman.

Skobelev didn't notice. He picked up his cup and sipped daintily. His gestures were like his clothes, tidy and perfect. A man to whom perfection was perhaps a god.

"It's simple, really," he said. "Only the best men should rule the world. Why do we have so many problems? So many wars? Because the wrong kind of people get into leadership roles. They're fooled into trusting nonexistent gods. Genetically and hormonally they're incapable of making intelligent decisions that will benefit everyone."

"And you are?" Anna said quietly, her face a brilliant red. Skobelev didn't even glance at her. But Blenkochev did. Again the warning look. She dropped her eyelashes.

"Of course!" Skobelev said confidently, his chest pushing against the white silk suit. "And that brings us to the issue of Carter."

He gazed at Blenkochev. He was issuing a challenge. What was to be done with the American spy?

Blenkochev looked coldly at Carter, and in that moment the AXE agent knew his usefulness to Blenkochev was over. He was abandoned.

"Do whatever you like," the KGB man said. He'd achieved his reputation for ruthlessness by crawling up over the corpses of his no-longer-useful comrades. "He knows little about your operation. And that means Hawk knows next to nothing." By abandoning Carter, he strengthened his position with Skobelev and Silver Dove.

"Then you're shortsighted," Carter said.

Everyone in the room turned to stare at Carter. Until he'd spoken, he was a piece of furniture. Now they remembered that he had a life and will of his own. A reputation. It made them edgy, even more eager to be rid of him, just as they would any potentially dangerous animal. Only Anna looked at him sympathetically. And she was as powerless as he.

"Take him away," Skobelev said, his fingers flicking with distaste at the AXE agent. "Kill him."

SIXTEEN

The heater in the corner across from Nick Carter hissed. The warm, stuffy office air stank of Leon Blenkochev's perfume. The hot eyes of the Soviet guards were focused on Carter, burning with the delightful prospect of killing him.

Two of the Silver Doves grabbed his arms.

Casually Carter shrugged, stepping between them.

Carter still didn't have the information he needed. His weapons were gone. It was too early to fight.

He wasn't surprised by Blenkochev's abandonment. When it was time, he'd have to figure a way to escape, but it wasn't time yet. His gaze swept the Soviets and settled on General Skobelev.

"You're planning some kind of biological warfare," Carter said. "But it won't do you any good. We've almost got the serum to combat it."

It was Skobelev's turn to shrug.

"I'm not impressed," the Silver Dove general said, "unless you have proof of your serum."

"No proof here, but I can tell you that the New Zealand doctors who treated the attaché and the Chilean soldier are working with our medical people. There'll be a breakthrough soon." Carter smiled, almost believing the lie. "Another miracle of modern medicine. By the end of the week."

Skobelev studied Carter only a moment. Confidence

surged through the general. His pastel, dandyish figure vibrated with it.

"Nonsense," the Silver Dove leader decided. "Take him!"

The guards' grip on Carter's arms tightened and they walked him to the door.

"When the entire world laughs at your threats you won't believe it's nonsense," Carter said.

He allowed a sneer into his voice.

A flush rose up the general's cheeks. He didn't want to be made a fool of. Still, he motioned to the guards, and they shoved Carter closer to the door.

"They'll say, 'The stupid Silver Dove . . . as out of date as a dinosaur!' " Carter laughed. " 'So behind the times they couldn't even win a mud-wrestling match!' Do you think anyone will listen to threats of biological warfare when the United States will share the serum freely with everyone?"

"Enough!" the general snapped.

Skobelev stood. He was ramrod straight, dignified against Carter's impossible accusations. He believed in himself so thoroughly that the disbelief of others only strengthened him.

He wasn't insane, not yet, but his unwillingness to reason had pushed him into fanaticism.

"Americans all have one common malady," the general observed hotly. "They think they're invincible. It will destroy them in the end!"

He opened the door behind his desk. His movements bristled with pride. He was totally involved with himself as he strode through the door and motioned to the guards to follow with their charge.

"I'll show you, Nick Carter!" he proclaimed. "Great Killmaster. Great fool!"

Carter smiled, a slow deep smile of satisfaction. Now perhaps he'd find out what was going on in the Silver Dove installation so well hidden inside the Antarctic mountain.

The laboratory on the other side of General Skobelev's

office was another enormous room. The air temperature was controlled, thermometers placed strategically over lab tables and equipment.

Glass and steel glistened under fluorescent lights. Culture dishes, bunsen burners, rows and rows of tubes and vials, electronic instruments, recorders, and white-smocked doctors and lab technicians—all males—filled the busy room. Carter had yet to see any other woman but Anna in the Silver Dove installation. Against the far wall, bright lights on computer consoles flashed on and off.

In the heart of the room's scientific array was a thick glass cage about ten feet by ten feet. Scientists worked outside the glass cage, their hands inside gloves. Each of their minute hand movements was copied exactly by the hand movements of corresponding robots inside the glass cage. The robots carried, poured, heated, and slid samples under microscopes—whatever the hands of the working scientists demanded.

"Very professional," Carter observed.

He stood inside the door with Skobelev, Blenkochev, Anna, and the guards. After glancing over their shoulders at the visitors, the scientists went on working.

Full of pride, Skobelev gazed at the scene.

"Of course," Skobelev said arrogantly. "This is where we developed the strain. SD-Forty-two."

"Silver Dove Forty-two," Anna murmured.

Skobelev looked at her briefly, then dismissed her from his mind. The presence of her sex was an irritation, a reminder of worldwide imperfection.

"And the original bacterium?" Carter said. "Was it found here?"

Skobelev waved his arm to encompass the mountain.

"Mutated and grown here," he said. "Soon we'll be ready! One of our cosmonauts stumbled on it in outer space. He kept it under sterile conditions until we had the lab here operating. It was easy to hide such a find in the layers of Russia's overweight bureaucracy."

"I suppose Rocky Diamond proved useful to you," Carter said grimly, imagining Diamond's painful death.

"The American aviator?" Skobelev said. "Yes. Such stamina. Still, he succumbed in twenty-four hours. That seems to be the maximum time needed for the bacteria to work. It was unfortunate for him that he had to land near here with engine trouble, and then that he saw my men. We grabbed him just as he was radioing out."

"And now?" Blenkochev asked. "Now that everything is ready, when do we move?"

The KGB leader appeared eager, as if he were truly a member of Silver Dove shaping a new future. Perhaps Blenkochev's joining hadn't been a ruse.

Carter looked at him carefully.

"Soon." Skobelev smiled. "Very soon, dear Blenkochev, we'll tell Chernenko and the others what we have here. Bacteriological warfare that will wipe out all the human lives it touches! They'll scream and complain, but they'll have no choice. They'll hand over control of Mother Russia. And with you and me joined, we'll rule Russia! I'll take the military, and you the government. Then, quickly, we'll force the nations of the world to the peace table, and great Mother Russia will benevolently rule the earth forever!"

"Ah!" said Blenkochev, beaming.

"I'm not convinced," Carter said. "Do you think the people who've struggled to power in their nations will capitulate so easily? Fighting for what they believe in is second nature. As soon as our serum is developed, your plan is dead."

Skobelev threw back his head and laughed. His pastel figure shook with merriment. At last he pulled the crimson handkerchief from his pocket and dabbed his eyes.

"Your serum is based on the Chilean soldier and the New Zealand attaché?" the Silver Dove leader asked, chuckling.

"Yes," Carter said.

"Then it's worthless!" Skobelev said. "Those two died of the *old* bacterial strain! The new one is the one that killed

Diamond. He stumbled into our hands just in time to be our first human guinea pig. It worked so well that we've discarded the others. The *new* strain is the one that we'll use to win the world. Your so-called serum is worthless!''

The cell Nick Carter was thrown in was cold and damp. It was a hole, blasted out of the granite mountain. The heavy steel door clanged shut, and he was in a semidarkness lit only by a hallway light through bars high on the door. Somewhere in the underground cells he heard women's voices, low, subdued, beaten.

He stood, stamped his feet, and walked around the cell. He had no equipment. His weapons and radio were gone. He needed to escape now, to inform Hawk of what he'd learned.

He paced the cell. It was furnished with a narrow cot, sink, and toilet. The smell of women lingered in it. He'd passed their cells as he was brought here.

Women weren't good enough in the Silver Dove compound for anything but sex. In the distance, one of them sang a keening song of sadness and betrayal. Locked in until called, kept on birth control powders mixed in with their food, they were here only for the Silver Doves' physical pleasure.

That pleasure was the women's single purpose in a life shortened by captivity and hopelessness. The Silver Doves' own women—their legal wives—would be home in Russia raising children and waiting for their heroic men.

Carter walked the length of the cell, then back again. The women talked. Water dripped somewhere. He could almost hear the motors of the vehicles in the warehouse entrance overhead. He could almost feel the cold fresh air of the Antarctic summer. For one brief moment he thought of trout jumping in high New Zealand lakes.

His gaze roamed the cell as if it, too, were a verdant wilderness humming with life and he were a man free to enjoy it.

Then his eyes stopped. In the granite wall to the left of the cell door one of the women had scratched "God save me. God save us all."

Footsteps echoed in the corridor outside Carter's cell. He walked to the door and stared out between the high bars. It was Anna. Limp. Unconscious. Her blond hair streamed down her blue snowsuit almost to the floor.

Two Silver Dove guards supported her under the armpits as they dragged her down the hall past Carter's cell.

"Where do we put her?" one of the guards said to the other in Russian.

"Anywhere there's room," said the other.

The second man was the Russian with the square face and the bushy black mustache. The man with whom—perhaps—Blenkochev had exchanged a silent sign of recognition when the group had first entered the Silver Dove installation.

"Skobelev wants her for himself," the first one said. "After the first time, she'll have her own cell."

"You can put her in here until then," Carter said from between his bars.

The two looked up over their shoulders and frowned.

"Blenkochev would like that," Carter went on. "His assistant. She'll have privacy here."

His gaze drifted to the mustachioed guard. Carter thought he saw a moment of thoughtful hesitation, a willingness to please Blenkochev. It might be the key out of the Silver Dove installation.

"And now that Blenkochev and Skobelev are partners," Carter continued, "well . . . I'm sure you can see why it's best to please *both* of the future rulers of the world."

The appeal to vanity and self-preservation worked on their thick faces.

"It might be best," the mustachioed guard said.

The other shrugged indifferently. The two wheeled Anna around and dragged her back to Carter's cell.

The door opened noisily, letting in the sad sounds of the distant captive women.

The men gestured Carter against the wall, then dropped Anna on the cot. As they turned to leave, their boots noisy on the granite floor, Carter stepped forward.

"What about first aid for her?" he said.

The first guard laughed and headed for the door, the other guard with the mustache close behind.

"She's more than Blenkochev's assistant," Carter said softly behind the second guard's back.

The mustachioed guard's boots worked noisily across the floor, hiding Carter's voice from the first guard. The man's shoulders tightened, but he didn't turn around.

"She's his daughter," Carter said. "Tell him where she is."

The bruise on Anna's forehead was big and red, enough to knock out a man twice her size. Carter held her in his arms, keeping her warm as he lay protectively on the cot with her. He didn't like to think of her joining the doomed women in the cells along the corridor.

From the size of her pupils, he believed she'd escaped a concussion. He would wait, and hope she awoke on her own. If she did, he would be more certain she was all right. There was nothing more he could do now.

She was a small woman, fitting comfortably against him. His body encircled hers as if they'd been together often. He thought about the way she'd looked at him before he'd gone into his tent on the flat, snowy land. He remembered the veiled desire, and then the thickening in his throat as he admired her blond beauty.

Her heartbeat was regular, her breath sweet. He brushed his lips against the fragrant silky hair and closed his eyes. She moaned and moved against him, a small hurt animal, sensuous without knowing it.

• • •

The kisses under his chin were light and feathery. The fingers traced the outlines of his ear. The lips moved up his neck, and deep warmth spread through him.

"Nick," she murmured.

"Anna, you're all right . . . ?"

Her lips fell on his mouth. Hungry. Demanding.

He pulled her into him. Her body melted, heated him with desire.

He swallowed the moisture in her mouth. Her tongue darted between his teeth, explored. Shivers of power coursed through him.

He stood her up and pulled off her parka. She pulled off his.

They undressed one another, standing, touching, feeling in the cold cell.

She was small-waisted with high large breasts glowing like ivory in the dim light. A beautiful woman all over.

Her lips parted, swollen with desire.

He cupped the perfect breasts, kissed the nipples. She threw back her head and arched her back.

"Oh, God!" she moaned.

He picked her up, feeling the promise of her hot in his arms.

She bit his neck and growled. Panting, Carter placed her on the cot.

She pulled him down, and he entered her.

They rocked together, as men and women have always joined, locked in the inescapable power of desire.

Later they lay entwined on the narrow cot, their clothes piled on them for warmth. She was a rough-and-tumble agent, believable disguised as a man, but in bed she was soft and fragrant, wearing her own kind of perfume that made Carter think of French wildflowers.

He kissed around the lump on her forehead.

"Still hurt?" he murmured.

"It's the only place that does." She smiled. "I feel so good. All over. I'm not even angry anymore."

"At Skobelev?"

"At all of them. The way they treat women, other minorities. The damned Silver Doves!"

"And your father?"

She was quiet a moment, then shrugged.

"He doesn't know I'm here. He went to lunch with Skobelev. 'Man talk.' " She sneered, clenching her fists. " 'A female wouldn't understand.' So I went to the canteen. Some of the men . . . wanted me. There was a fight. I . . . got a couple. Then someone got me."

"One of the doves who brought you said that Skobelev wanted you."

She looked at him.

"Skobelev?" she said, lips curling. "Me?"

"I take it you'd rather pass."

The edges of her mouth curled in a smile. Then she laughed.

"He's ridiculous! How could anyone want him?"

"He doesn't think he's ridiculous. He thinks he's going to run the world. With the help of your father."

She was silent. She gazed around the granite cell.

"We don't have any equipment," she said shortly. "How are we going to get out?"

"You don't know whether your father's turned," he said, watching her beautiful regular features.

Her expression didn't change.

"He's not my father here," she said. "He's Leon Blenkochev, the great head of the feared KGB agency K-GOL. He gives me orders, and I don't question him."

"He could have fooled us both, and betrayed his country. Your country."

She closed her eyes.

"I don't know what to do," she admitted.

He stroked the long pale hair. She sighed, resting her

forehead against his neck. Her breath was warm against his skin.

"There's nothing more we can do now," he said. "Only wait."

She tipped back her head and gazed deep into his eyes.

"I wanted you the first time I saw you," she said softly. "Back in New Zealand."

She took his hand and moved it to her round breast. He cupped it, touched the nipple, and it rose erect.

He kissed her, then pulled her close, crushing her against him as he felt his own heat rise hot and hard.

The door lock rattled. The key turned.

She pushed away from him, eyes wide with sudden terror.

"Skobelev!" she hissed. "I won't go with him! I won't!"

SEVENTEEN

Naked, Nick Carter ran across the granite cell and stood behind the door. He heard only one man outside. Still on the cot, Anna Blenkochev pulled on clothes and quickly took stock of the cell, alert and ready.

The door swung open.

Carter counted to three, then slammed back against it.

The visitor went flying, landing with a thud against the outside corridor wall.

Carter pulled the door open. Anna threw his clothes at him.

She ran past him into the corridor, looking both ways for danger.

"Come on!" she whispered. "Hurry!"

"Wait!" he said, grabbing her arm. "Do you know him?"

They stared at the square-faced Silver Dove with the bushy black mustache.

"I . . . I think so . . ."

She walked forward.

"Lev Larionov. He's an Orthodox priest. Or at least he used to be."

"Back in the cell," Carter said, and he picked up the limp man.

Carter put Larionov on the cot while Anna closed the door. The newcomer groaned and rolled his head.

"I wonder what he's doing here," Anna said as she tried the door to make sure it hadn't relocked.

"I suspect your father planted him," Carter said as he dressed. "He'd want his own people in each of the KGB's undergroups. Now my question is why Larionov came back."

"Blenkochev . . . sent me . . ." Larionov said weakly. "I'm glad . . . you told me."

He grabbed the wall behind the cot and pulled himself up. Anna sat on the cot beside him.

"Can you get us out of here?" Carter said.

"Told you what?" Anna said, confused.

"Carter sent me to tell your father where you were," Larionov said, holding his head. "And I'm going to try to get you out."

She looked at the AXE agent.

"You trusted my father when even I didn't," she said, her eyes full of wonder.

"I know his reputation," Carter said. "He's smoothest at double-crossing. Now he's double-crossing Skobelev's Silver Doves. But he doesn't trust easily either. He couldn't trust us to know for sure what he was up to." He looked at the former priest. "We'd better leave."

Larionov nodded, then made the sign of the cross.

"I'll be glad when this assignment is over," he said.

He stood, and opened and closed his eyes. They were bright now; gone was the dull, stupid look he'd assumed earlier as a Silver Dove.

"Blenkochev wants you to come back with reinforcements," Larionov said.

"He's not leaving here?" Anna said. "Then I won't go."

"It's not safe for you here," Carter agreed. "You've said too much. Skobelev knows you fundamentally disagree with him."

"And Skobelev will keep you locked up down here with the others," Larionov warned. "Blenkochev can't help you without endangering the mission. He orders you to leave."

She blanched, wringing her hands in her lap as she understood the situation.

"You have no choice," Carter told her gently. Then he looked at the square-faced Larionov. "You have a hidden radio that I can contact you on?"

Larionov nodded and gave Carter the frequency. Then the priest opened the door and checked outside. He disappeared for a moment and returned with a sack.

"Two air rifles," Larionov explained. "There'll be survival supplies in the skimobile."

He gave them directions as Carter and Anna checked the weapons.

"They'll think we stole these along the way," Carter said, opening the door. "Lie where you fell, Larionov. You've got a bruise on your head. No need to hit you again."

"You'll help my father?" Anna asked as the former priest slid down the corridor wall.

"Of course," Larionov said simply. "We all must stop Silver Dove. Whether we believe in God or not, we must believe in people's right to choose."

Carter and Anna ran down the hall, past the faceless cell doors and the keening women, over the rough granite.

As they approached a sharp corner, they slowed. Larionov had warned them that floor-to-ceiling bars, a locked door, and a guard waited on the other side.

They peered around the granite wall's edge. Beyond were plasterboard walls, forced-air heat, the locked, barred door, and not one guard, but three. So far, only one of Larionov's predictions was wrong.

Two of the three men were leaning against a wall, smoking. The third sat in front of a metal desk, drinking coffee. They talked in loud voices, telling stories and jokes. They were totally involved with themselves, oblivious to the faint sounds of the locked-up, weakened women.

Their air rifles were across their arms. Two were right-handed; the third was left-handed. Their belts were loaded with knives, walkie-talkies, keys, saps, and brass knuckles. An unused arsenal that made them feel like men.

"What will we do?" Anna whispered.

"No time and no choice," Carter said. He needed them alive, needed at least one of them healthy enough to unlock the cell door.

He motioned her back behind him, then raised his rifle. He aimed and shot two of them in the right arm and the third in the left before any of the three had a chance to raise his own weapon and retaliate.

The wounded men shouted with surprise and pain. Their air rifles fell clattering to the floor. Blood splattered briefly, a fine spray that quickly dispersed into the air as red pools spread across their arms.

"Unlock the door!" Carter ordered.

One man dived for his air rifle.

Another scrambled behind the desk, preparing to bolt down the hall to safety.

Carter shot the Silver Dove air rifle as the man reached for it. It skidded across the floor.

He shot above the desk, sending metal slivers into the air, a warning.

"Unlock the door!" Carter again ordered.

The third Silver Dove narrowed his eyes at Carter.

Suddenly a knife flew from behind the desk.

Carter ducked.

The knife slammed uselessly against the granite wall behind Carter.

Carter crouched.

"Don't!" he warned, but the Silver Doves weren't to be so easily stopped.

The man with the narrow eyes had his walkie-talkie out and was scuttling behind the desk to safety. The one who'd gone after his air rifle now had it. And the one behind the desk stood up suddenly and ran down the hall.

As shots rang around him, Carter fired at the Dove who was escaping. The man stumbled and fell, blood pouring from wounds in each leg.

Carter dropped flat on the floor, a smaller target, and fired at the Dove with the walkie-talkie. The walkie-talkie exploded into a thousand pieces.

He fired at last at the rash Dove with the air rifle who was squatting unsheltered against the plaster wall. He put a neat hole in the man's shoulder, then shot the air rifle into another slide across the hall.

The defeated Doves looked at Carter with amazement.

"Unlock this goddamned door!" he ordered.

Now they looked at one another, then the one who'd lost the walkie-talkie crept to the door, never taking his eyes off Carter's air rifle.

He unlocked the door and backed off.

Disgusted, Carter walked through, then rounded up the men against the desk. Anna found rope, and the two agents quickly tied the three guards and sped off down the hall.

Carefully they rounded corners, sometimes having to wait or dashing into an empty room until the hall cleared. They passed through a section of sleeping quarters, behind the clutter of the massive kitchen, and along a row of offices where typewriters clattered and telephones rang. Lev Larionov's directions were good. Their biggest worry was remaining undiscovered.

Just as they entered a back door into the warehouse entry-way, the alarm went off.

It was a piercing scream amplified by loudspeakers throughout the complex.

Silver Doves in their white snowsuits and coveralls driving trucks, working on jeeps, carrying clipboards, and looking over manifests jerked to attention and grabbed their weapons.

The piercing scream continued.

Unnoticed, Carter and Anna edged along the wall to the bank of skimobiles. The enormous jaws of the warehouse doors were slowly closing. Anything that big took a while to move. Snow flurries showed beyond the doors. It could be another storm.

"Ready?" Carter said, jumping into the skimobile Larionev had told them to take.

Anna nodded, and Carter turned on the motor, a small noise compared to the alarm's torturous complaint. The opening to the outside world had grown smaller.

He turned the wheel, and the skimobile dashed down the center of the busy warehouse. He was relying on surprise.

The Silver Doves were surprised, but stubborn and well trained as well.

They raised their air rifles and fired.

Crouching, Anna fired back while Carter pushed the skimobile to speeds greater than it was built for.

Shots whizzed around them, hitting the metal sides of the skimobile.

The big doors' opening grew smaller.

Carter pressed on while Anna fired.

They rounded a group of trucks amid a hail of fire and sped toward the closing doors.

The opening was so narrow that the skimobile's sides brushed against it as they passed through.

Air rifle fire and shouts followed them through the opening, then the automatic doors closed. It would be a while before the Silver Doves could reopen them.

They were alone in sudden, dense silence.

For the moment, they were safe from the fanatics in the secret installation. Now they faced perhaps a greater foe— the Antarctic weather.

In the open skimobile, the icy air slashed at them as they sped down the valley. They did up their clothes as snowflakes whipped like streamers in the wind. The sky was clouded over gray and brown. It looked like a developing blizzard, but there was nothing to be done. They had to go on.

Anna opened a compartment in front of them and quickly

searched until she found a radio. Her fingers were red and wet.

"You're hurt!" Carter said.

She shrugged, pulled on mittens, and went to work on the radio.

"It's nothing," she said. "Anyway, there's nothing to be done about it now."

"Where?" he asked, worried.

"Thigh."

She put headphones over her ears, listened, then talked. Carter leaned over and saw Anna's wound. Her blood-soaked blue snowsuit would freeze soon.

"The radio doesn't work," she said.

"I'm not surprised. Once the weather lifts, it'll be okay."

He glanced at her and saw the drawn face. She was shaking with the bitter cold. The skimobile was wide open. No protection at all.

"Either you take care of that wound now or I stop here and do it myself."

She reached behind them and dug through their gear. She pulled a thermal blanket over her lap, tucked her legs in, and opened a first aid kit. At last she pulled the blanket up and poured antibiotic powder through her snowsuit into the rifle hole. She bit her lip.

"Bullet still in there?"

"Yes."

She wrapped gauze bandages around the leg. They'd have to wait to take the bullet out. If they tried now, hypothermia would set in and she would literally freeze to death. She needed to keep warm, and not move so that she didn't bleed so much.

A beginning fever reddened her cheeks and glazed her eyes. She pulled a knit balaclava over her face.

"Where to?" she said bravely.

"We'll never make Novolazarevskaya in this weather. We'll try to get out of the mountains and find my helicopter.

We can tent it and stay warm there.'' He needed to keep her warm.

They drove on into the brutal Antarctic, the blizzard slowly growing in intensity. She kept the insulated blanket wrapped around her. Still she shook with the cold and fever. Worried, helpless, Carter watched her as he did the only thing he could do—forge ahead.

EIGHTEEN

In the skimobile, Nick Carter and Anna Blenkochev traveled back down the valley, around, and up to the sheer mesa where the Silver Doves had captured them.

From there, using his trained memory and the traces of their old ski trail, Carter backtracked in the thickening snow flurries.

They traveled for hours, the brown-gray skies not yet opening to blast them with the threatened blizzard. The sunlight was hazy, the conditions bad. Mounds of snow stood frozen in dull diamondlike crystals, statues of immobility. The visibility lessened.

Anna's head fell back against the seat.

"Don't go to sleep!" Carter warned her.

"I won't," she said. "I'm just so tired."

"Sit up."

He shook her shoulder. She rolled her head to the side and looked at him.

"Come on, sit up!" he said.

She struggled up.

"Talk to me," he commanded.

In a halting voice she told him about Russia, about Moscow where she had grown up. Saint Basil's Cathedral of onion domes. Lenin's tomb. The Kremlin. Gorki Park. Slowly her voice strengthened with interest. About music lessons, violin concertos. About the mother who raised her while the absent father came to stay occasionally on weekends. She talked on as the snow thickened and the cold Antarctic day closed around them like a fist.

"And then, one day, he appeared with his suitcase and said he was home for good," she said, wonder in her voice. "After that, he was home most nights. I was like other little girls. I had both a mother and a father."

"She must be remarkable, your mother."

"Yes." She smiled.

"Someone he met while working?"

"Probably another reason why I'm an agent too."

"No one in my government knew he was even married. He kept her secret, and you, too. There's a reason for that," Carter said thoughtfully. "Is she a foreigner?"

Anna smiled broadly.

"I suppose it doesn't hurt to tell now. It's been so many years."

"American?" Carter's voice was incredulous.

"Leslee Warner. She was with AXE."

They drove on. Carter could feel her laugh quietly beside him. A family joke.

"Blenkochev would never have married an American unless he had good reason to trust her," Carter said. "Did she save his life?"

"Maybe." Anna smiled. "She saved him at least from imprisonment. Your Hawk had captured him and turned him over to other agents to take back to your country for questioning. She was one of the other agents. Everyone thought he killed her while escaping."

Again Anna leaned back against the seat.

"So that's how he got away," he said. "I never knew."

Carter contemplated the radical swing of events that occurred when human emotions became involved. How much information the United States had lost because one woman had lost her heart to the source of information.

And Blenkochev must have loved her, too, or else he'd

never have bothered to marry her. Instead, she would have been imprisoned in a Moscow cold-water flat and pumped dry, then exiled to a labor camp in Siberia.

Now she lived in bureaucratic luxury in a Moscow apartment and had a *dacha* for weekends and the summer overlooking the Moscow River. No wonder Blenkochev was always aware of how tenuous his position was. He must have pulled strings, bribed, and threatened to keep her from the fate of most captive foreign agents in Russia. There would be a dozen jealous, grudge-bearing bureaucrats waiting to depose him first chance they could.

"Is she happy?" Carter asked.

"Restless, but happy as any of us," Anna said, her heavy-lidded eyes closing.

"Dammit, Anna! Sit up!"

"I'm sorry," she said feebly. She struggled up again.

Her lips were blue surrounded by the face mask. They shivered with cold and fever.

Ahead the ribbons of snow had thickened into curtains. The wind howled along the top of the ridge they traveled. The skimobile rocked with the gales as if slapped around by the hand of a giant.

"I can't see much," Anna said, peering ahead. She gripped the skimobile to keep from being thrown out.

"Neither can I," Carter said grimly. "We'll have to stop. Did you find a snow tent in the gear?"

"In back," she said. "I feel as if we've been here before."

"It's the same trail," Carter said. "I want to go on a little farther, back to that sheltered spot where I put up the tents."

She nodded, sitting upright, her eyes closed.

"Anna!"

The eyes flew open.

His fingers were numb in the mittens. His lips were stiff. He had that queasy, hopeless feeling that came as cold relentlessly settled into the bones and marrow. They would have to stop and make camp soon.

"At least Silver Dove won't follow us in this weather," he

said. "They'll hope we die in it."

He watched as best he could. He saw the ridges and boulders he'd seen before, now covered with swirling mantles of snow. They made progress too slowly.

Then as the storm at last built itself into a fury, he saw what he wanted. Straight ahead. The boulders that spilled into a roof over the flat area.

He drove under the sheltering rock canopy and jumped out.

"Get out, Anna. Walk around. Now!"

Obediently she stumbled out as he pulled apart the gear on the back of the skimobile. With clumsy fingers he spread out the tent, pounded stakes, fitted the poles of its internal skeleton together, and inserted the skeleton into the tent. He was shaking with the cold. Anna stood dumbly nearby.

He attached a cord to the skimobile engine and made adjustments. He carried the other end of the cord and a bundle of supplies into the tent.

"Get in!" he told her.

She moved stiffly and slowly.

He picked her up and carried her. Inside the tent, he wrapped around her the special electric blanket that was plugged into the skimobile.

"This will warm you," he told her. "We'll take care of the bullet when you're strong enough."

He went back out to the skimobile, staked it down, stripped it of supplies, and carried them into the tent. Anna lay passively, her eyes closed. Her skin temperature was still dangerously low. She needed something hot inside her.

He heated soup above a solid-fuel pellet, held her head, and spooned it into her mouth as she swallowed feebly.

At last she licked her lips and sighed.

He drank soup until he felt hot and full.

He crawled into the heated blanket bag with her, pulled off his clothes and hers, and cradled her still-cold naked body against his.

●   ●   ●

The next day, the savage blizzard still groaning and howling outside the tent, Carter gave Anna a large dose of sleeping sedatives.

As she went to sleep, he heated antiseptic above the fuel pellet. He dropped in his knife and the forceps from the first aid box.

He adjusted the heated blanket so that her thigh wound was exposed to the cold air. He washed the skin. It was a ragged hole, but it was in the fleshy part of the leg. The bullet had missed her bone.

He laid out thread and needle, antibiotics, and gauze bandages. Then he used the sterilized knife to make the incision.

Blood poured out. He'd have to work quickly. He cut again, and inserted the forceps. Sweat beaded on his cold forehead. Anna cried out in her sleep.

At last he felt the hardness of the pellet. He turned the forceps, closed them over it, and pulled. Anna cried weakly.

Blood covered his hand, hot and sticky. He packed antibiotics into the wound. Sewed. Bandaged. His hands made gentle pressure to stem the bleeding.

He looked at her twisted face, the tears streaming down uncontrolled in her sleep. The twisted face of pain. Thank God she was unconscious.

He washed the instruments, cleaned up, and hoped.

After almost twelve hours of restless sleep, Anna awoke. Her face was gray.

"I was dreaming of the Englishman Scott," she said. "He was dragging a dog sled alone across an ice shelf. The dog sled was empty. No supplies. Totally useless to him. But he wouldn't give it up. It would be the death of him."

Carter watched her, worried.

"How do you feel?" he said.

"Weak," she said. "I didn't know getting shot could make you feel so terrible."

He made soup and they drank it quietly. She closed her eyes again and slept as the blizzard roared and crashed outside the shelter of their tent.

She awoke five more times over the next two days. Each time she claimed she felt better, but Carter could see that she had improved little if at all. Her skin color was bad. She had a fever. The wound had a puffy red ridge of infection around it. He opened it up and poured more antibiotics in, and insisted that she take oral antibiotics as well. Rather than argue, she did what he told her.

At the end of the third day she drank her soup heartily and asked for more. He gave it to her, pleased, and urged her to take as much as she could.

"Did you hear about Vostok Station, what happened in the winter of 1982?" she asked, peering over the top of her cup.

"Russian station," he said. "The power plant was destroyed by fire, as I recall."

"That's right. There were twenty men. They survived by using diesel fuel candles and an ice drill generator for power. There wasn't enough heat for everything. Just about all their equipment froze. But despite the hardships, they continued their scientific observations and extended the deep ice core hole they were studying. Rescuers didn't arrive until eight months had passed. Once Antarctica is frozen in for the winter, it's unreachable."

"It's summer now," Carter reminded her.

She looked at the sides of the tent, and watched them shudder and shake. She listened to the power of the brutal wind.

"We're unreachable right now," she said, putting her cup down. "How long have we been here?"

He told her, and she sighed.

"I'm holding you back," she said. "Without me, you'd go on."

"I'd be an idiot to go anywhere now. No one can see anything out there. I need shelter just like you do."

But still, she was right. He'd been thinking of the Silver Dove installation for all of the four days they'd been stranded there. Worried that Skobelev had already implemented the plan to contact Russia. Worried that an accident had happened and bacteria had escaped the lab to harm the world. Even worried that Skobelev had blamed Blenkochev for their escape and executed him. Carter needed Blenkochev safe inside the installation, needed him to help. But even Carter couldn't go on just yet. He had to wait for the blizzard to break. Then he would have to go slowly and carefully because of Anna. Even with the skimobile, he'd have to rest more often to care for her. He didn't want anything else to happen to her.

She was looking at him, staring deep into his eyes.

He smiled.

"Come here," she said. "Take off your clothes and come inside with me."

Her eyes were sapphire blue, as bright as her flaxen hair. He ran his hand from her blond crown to the tips of the soft, silky strands. He kissed the fragrant hair.

"I want you," she said simply.

Her eyes were tender now, smiling, as shining as stars.

He wanted her, too, the passion growing big within him.

As she watched, her eyes hungry, he took off his clothes and slid inside the blanket.

She wrapped her arms around his neck, melting into him, the bandaged leg strong and firm against him.

He kissed her, and she ran her fingers down his chest, kneading his sides, insistent.

He buried his face in her hair, while they touched, tasting the salt and sweetness of the other. Felt the intimate places that made them soar. They made love, building to their peaks as leisurely as if the world stood still for them.

Later, Carter slept the sleep of the exhausted. The last few days weighed heavily upon him: the constant observation and care of Anna; the constant worry and planning about the Silver Doves' activities; the frustration that he couldn't be out and doing something about it. But now he was happy, exhausted but happy in the way all men are when they're with the right woman.

When he awoke, she was gone.
The sleeping bag was empty. The tent was empty.
Shock of what it meant set in.
Naked, he ran into the howling wind.
''Anna! Anna!''
There was no answer.

NINETEEN

Naked, Nick Carter couldn't pursue Anna. He ran back into the tent, threw on clothes, and raced back outside. He stared into the thick whiteness. There was no sign of her. There wouldn't be. She'd see to that, and the storm would help. The blizzard poured a curtain of thick wet flakes down. The wind hurled snow back up from the ground. The temperature must have been forty below zero.

He struggled through drifts, making wider arcs around the tent. She could have been gone eight hours. With the right conditions, she'd have been dead in fifteen minutes.

He forced his way on, the tent fading in and out of the sheets of whiteness. The cold pierced his bones. He pushed the danger from his mind. She'd left so that he could move swiftly to complete the mission. The dream about Scott's empty dog sled, the remarks that she was holding him back, all came back to haunt Carter. He shuddered and stumbled on, hoping, searching for the bright blue snowsuit.

Then he fell into the drift.

It was soft, wet, like quicksand sucking him deeper and deeper. He clawed the snow, coughed for air. He felt himself sinking into oblivion. It was easy. He was tired, and it was very easy just to stay in the womb of snow. And die.

He jerked with the thought. His mind had grown sluggish with the cold. Soon he wouldn't care.

He struggled, found the rock ledge that the drift sided, and pushed up through the snow. He made his arms and legs work until he emerged, clawing his way out to lie on the surface, panting.

He couldn't stay there. Had to go on. Find Anna. He rolled off the drift and stumbled to his feet. Where next? Where had he come from?

He looked around. He didn't know. He was going to die because he didn't know. And Silver Dove would complete their plan to take over the world.

With all his tremendous will, the Killmaster forced himself to focus his numb mind. He had to get back to the tent or perish. He had to accept Anna's sacrifice.

Then he saw it. The brief shine of chrome. The skimobile. The curtain of white closed, but Carter held the direction steady in his mind and, stunned and grieving, fought his way back to the shelter of the tent.

The next day, the blizzard stopped. Stone-cold silence enveloped the lonely tent. Immediately Carter tried the radio. All he got was static. He dressed and went outside.

She'd taken nothing with her. She'd put on her blue snow-suit and walked away. Any direction. As far away as she could get. Where he couldn't find her. Couldn't rescue her.

He went to the skimobile and kicked it. Once. Twice. He wanted to throw it over the side of the mountain. He wanted to smash the mountain into a million pieces and hurl them into the face of the merciless gods.

Instead, the AXE agent packed supplies and took down the tent. He loaded everything onto the skimobile. He knew where he was going. He'd planned the shortest, quickest route to the closest base that he was sure he could trust.

He started the motor and drove off, Anna's beautiful face with the flowing flaxen hair set forever in his mind.

Northeast of the Antarctic Peninsula on the Weddell Sea

sat the cereal-box structures of the United Kingdom's Halley Station. After a loss of funding during the fighting on the Falkland Islands, the station again pulsed with activity, much of it centered on new high-speed satellite communications equipment and a new geophysical observatory.

It was a clear Antarctic day, the sun gleaming above the horizon. Assorted scientists and maintenance crew walked and rode around the snowy compound, checking for damage caused by the blizzard.

Inside a quiet office, alerted at last by Carter's helicopter radio, sat David Hawk and Chester ffolkes, their faces grim.

"Sorry about Anna," Hawk said. He pulled a cigar from his pocket and stared at it thoughtfully. "Blenkochev and Leslee Warner. Their daughter. Must have been a damned fine agent." He looked up at Carter. "You thought a lot of her. It happens."

"So *that's* how that bloody bastard got away, David," ffolkes said and smiled. The gold on his teeth shone in the overhead lights. "He never did take the usual way out. And all these years we thought he'd killed poor Leslee. Sorry she ended up in Moscow. Boring place. Gray. They say Siberia's worse, but I don't believe it. I suppose that's what she gets for defecting."

Hawk nodded and lit the cigar. His cheeks bellowed as he drew it to life. He looked at Carter, waiting.

"I've radioed Lev Larionov," Carter reported. "He'll relay the plan to Blenkochev and tell him about Anna. Her death should keep him in line, although I think he's sincere about not wanting General Skobelev and the Silver Doves in power."

"A bit ticklish," ffolkes said, "breaking into a place that manufactures bacteria for biological warfare. We'll need all three of you. We'll have the troops ready by the time you get there."

Carter nodded. His thoughts, energy, and emotions were now focused on only one thing: the mission.

"Good luck, Nick," Hawk said solemnly. "I'm afraid you'll need it."

Mike Strange was waiting for him in the little nuclear helicopter. Her face was flushed pink with excitement. A ski cap hid her chestnut hair, only a few glossy strands blowing in the breeze.

"I'll pilot," she said happily. "God! It's so good to be out!"

Her enthusiasm made him smile.

"All right," he said. "Glad you're well again. We'll head toward Novolazarevskaya. I found a place we can land that's close to the Silver Dove installation."

She turned on the helicopter, listened with satisfaction to its noise.

"And our antiterrorist backup troops?" she said.

"They'll be flown in from the opposite direction. Americans, New Zealanders, English, and Russians through Blenkochev's Silver Dove sleeper. An international force to solve a global problem. They'll wait hidden outside on skimobiles. Our job is to sneak in, seize General Skobelev, and isolate the lab. If the timing's right, the units will be able to come in then and take care of the rest of the Silver Doves before the Doves get us."

She looked at him, her dark eyes worried.

"There are so many things that can go wrong," she said.

"Too many," he agreed.

"And if we can't prevent one of the fanatics from setting free some lethal bacteria?"

"Then it won't matter," Carter said somberly. "We're all dead anyway."

Silently involved with their own thoughts and worries, they flew up into the glassy Antarctic air, over the snow and rock of Coats Land into Queen Maud Land and toward the mountains that rimmed the Princess Astrid Coast. Alert, they watched the skies for Silver Dove aircraft.

Ahead, the mountains where the Silver Dove installation

was concealed rose raw and rocky, the snow settled fluffy and innocent as clouds into valleys and crevasses. Somewhere in those snowy depths brave Anna's body was buried.

"I'm sorry about her," Mike said at last. "Anna Blenkochev. Rotten break."

"Yes."

They flew above a pair of snow petrels, hardy Antarctic birds that nest on mountain crags as much as two hundred miles inland, and then above a striated caracara, dark and hawklike, one of the world's rarest birds of prey. The two agents flew on as the sun slowly circled the horizon and shadows moved like sluggish wraiths across the sparkling, rocky earth.

They landed on the flatlands where Carter and Anna had camped. The marks of their tent and skimobile were still there.

While Mike unleashed the new skimobile from the back of the helicopter, Carter walked in widening arcs around the area. He knew it was hopeless, but he had to be sure. And he wanted to give Anna's body a proper burial.

But there was no sign of her. Snow from the blizzard was piled an additional fifteen feet in some places. He covered the entire flat area and then ranged around the rim. She couldn't have gotten any farther in the thick, bitter storm. He remembered stories of some bodies being found thirty years after they'd been lost in Antarctic blizzards.

"Nick!" Mike called. "Let's go!"

It was over. Anna was dead, and he wouldn't find her body. It was unrealistic to think otherwise. He needed to put her out of his mind. Get back to the living. Get back to the vital work he had to do.

He slogged back toward the skimobile, and Mike met him in it halfway. Her vibrant face watched him compassionately.

"I'll drive," he told her.

She nodded, sliding across the seat. He hopped in, and felt the wheel hum under his hands. It was a familiar sensation.

Machinery at work. Reliable. Trustworthy. Depending on you for care. But without emotion and passion. What made humanity special. Why he loved his work, making a better world for people.

He smiled, turned the skimobile, and headed back the familiar trail toward the Silver Dove installation.

"Keep close watch," he warned Mike. "The Doves will be out patrolling. And they wear white suits. It's almost impossible to see against the snow and ice."

She nodded, then glanced at her and Carter's khaki snow clothing.

"But when our antiterrorist troups go to work," she said, "they'll at least be able to tell us and themselves from the Silver Doves."

"That's the idea."

Skillfully Carter drove the skimobile along the trail, along ridges, over crests, between slopes, and down valleys as they drew closer and closer to the mountain that housed the Silver Doves.

At last Carter stopped the machine. He gestured for Mike to put on her cross-country skis, and he put on his. With backpacks and ski poles, they silently, stealthily made their way on a new path that Carter hoped—

Suddenly he raised the special air rifle that Lev Larionov had given him so long ago in the Doves' dungeon. He had to be quick before he was spotted.

Mike's eyebrows went up with surprise. She looked around for a target.

Carter shot across a wide gorge. The shot made a dull, quiet sound.

Mike's gaze followed the line of his trajectory. Across from them, a tall figure dressed all in white suddenly stood, grasping his chest. He was far enough away that he was as small as a child's doll. He let out a low cry of pain and toppled down over the high mesa, spinning end over end, until he landed silently below, almost invisible in the snow.

"One of the sentries?" Mike said, impressed.

Carter nodded grimly.

"The one who radioed the Dove headquarters for reinforcements when Anna, Blenkochev, and I wanted to be captured," he said. "One of the reasons to let yourself be captured at a secret base is to get enough information so that you can break in later undetected."

"It's a dangerous way to get the information."

"But sometimes it's the only way," he said. "Now we can backtrack and follow the trail for a while with less chance of discovery. On the other side of that mesa is the valley where the Silver Doves have dug in."

They skied back and around to the sheer rock wall where they could look down. Mike watched the white stick figures below through binoculars.

"They'd be impossible to see from the air," she murmured. "They may be bigots, but they're smart ones."

She handed the binoculars back to Carter. He tucked them into his backpack and checked his watch.

"Sixty-four minutes," he said. "Should be plenty of time."

She smiled, and they skied silently down the mountain. They stopped behind a house-size boulder. They could hear the noisy motors of trucks and jeeps not far away.

They took off their skis and backpacks, opened the backpacks, and unfolded white suits made by personnel at Valley to fit Carter's description. The two agents put the snowsuits on over their khaki suits. Each white suit had a silver dove embroidered over the heart.

They dug a hole in the snowdrift behind them and buried their backpacks. They stepped into their white cross-country skis and locked them to their boots. They slung the authentic Silver Dove air rifles over their shoulders, pulled white ski masks down over their hair and faces, and like two sentries returning for dinner, they skied around two behemoth boulders and into the Silver Dove valley.

Carter looked at his watch.

"Thirty-three minutes," he told Mike.

She checked her own watch and nodded.

They skied on as white jeeps and trucks carrying construction crews and boxes drove sedately on the packed-snow road. Boulders had been bulldozed aside. A taped Russian folk tune played from someone's skimobile.

The two disguised agents skied on toward the massive doors that opened into the Silver Dove installation. None of the valley workers looked at Carter and Mike with more than idle curiosity, probably grateful they didn't have the boring job of sentry.

Tension growing, using the information his careful observations had given him, Carter and Mike skied through the doors and into the exhaust-filled warehouse. Inside the tall doors they took off their skis and put them over their shoulders.

"Twenty-one minutes," he told her.

They carried their skis and ski poles past the rows of vehicles and workers, Carter leading, Mike silently behind toward the doors hewn into the granite.

There Carter stopped and lifted his ski mask to encircle his head. Mike did the same, her long chestnut hair hidden beneath the remaining cap. Without makeup, walking with her shoulders swinging rather than with her hips, a stern expression on her usually radiant face, she looked masculine enough to pass a superficial visual examination.

They left their skis propped against the rough granite wall, took off their mittens, and went through the door into the heated hallway. Their quiet, efficient, and safe passage couldn't continue forever.

They walked down the hall past clattering typewriters and ringing telephones. Office workers in white slacks and shirts moved back and forth across the hall carrying clipboards and sheaves of papers.

Carter and Mike looked straight ahead, businesslike. They were two ordinary sentries on the way back to their bunks.

They continued down the hall, around corners, toward the door of General Yevgeny Skobelev's office. Carter checked his watch.

"Fifteen minutes," Carter muttered under his breath to Mike.

She nodded, whistling tunelessly.

They stopped at a water fountain and drank, people passing up and down the hall.

In a short lull, the hall briefly empty, they swung their air rifles into their hands.

"Twelve minutes," Carter said.

They were cutting it close. But if they had no problems, the timing would be perfect.

Weapons aimed straight ahead, Carter opened Skobelev's door.

"Drop the guns!" Skobelev ordered harshly.

He held Carter's Luger, Wilhelmina, and it was aimed directly at Carter's heart. Carter could kill Skobelev. A shot through the head and it would be over. But he needed Skobelev, and time was running out.

TWENTY

A dozen White Doves poured in through the two doors that led to the hall and laboratory. They brandished their weapons at the agents, surrounding them with leers and the potential of instant death.

"Don't look so surprised, Killmaster," Skobelev said with satisfaction. "We've been tracking you since you killed our sentry. Did you think we didn't expect you back?" He laid Carter's Luger on the desk and dusted an imaginary speck from its shining barrel. "You must appreciate your reputation. If the blizzard didn't kill you, we could assume no less than your return."

"You monitored the sentries," Carter said.

"Exactly, my bright Killmaster," Skobelev said, beaming with approval. It was a pleasure killing a worthy opponent. "All the sentries were fixed with special electronic devices. When one of their hearts stopped, the appropriate light lit up on the computer next door. After that, it was easy. We knew how you'd be coming in, and could watch you."

Carter nodded thoughtfully, seemingly impressed.

"That's my Luger," Carter said, gesturing at the gun on Skobelev's desk.

"I know," the general said with satisfaction. "I have all your equipment."

"Not quite all," Carter said, his turn to be pleased.

He flexed his knee, and the pin to a small gas bomb, twin to Pierre, popped out. The bomb dropped quietly from his pant leg onto the floor as all the Silver Doves trained their attention on their leader and Nick Carter.

"Nine minutes," Mike said softly beside him. "Better speed it up."

"What?" Skobelev said, irritated. "Speak up! You're going to be dead soon anyway. This is your last chance to talk—"

The bomb hissed loudly and exploded with the deadly, odorless gas. Carter and Mike held their breaths, waiting, counting. It took only thirty seconds for a person to fall unconscious from the gas, another thirty seconds for them to die if not removed to safe air.

"Carter!" Skobelev shouted. "What's he done? Nikolai? Alexei? What's he done!?"

Skobelev stood up and leaned over his desk to see.

Confused, the Silver Doves hesitated, looking at one another. Several of them sniffed the air, unsure.

"It's a bomb!" Skobelev yelled. "Grab it!"

One of the Doves bolted for safety through the office door into the hall. Three others followed.

Two braver ones ducked to grab the bomb and throw it out after the cowards.

The rest of the Doves turned on Carter.

Unmoving, not breathing, not wanting to attract any more attention to himself, Carter watched their fingers flex on their triggers. Their adrenaline was raging. They'd be breathing faster, harder. Then he saw their eyes flicker. Their bodies sway. They took even deeper breaths. Their eyes glazed.

In unison, Carter and Mike reached up under their caps and pulled down small gas masks to cover their noses and mouths.

The scream of the alarm reverberated through the installation. The Silver Doves who'd escaped the office had turned it on.

Skobelev lifted heavy eyes to look out the door. He fell over his desk. One by one, the other Doves in the room collapsed.

Carter and Mike jumped over the bodies. They grabbed Skobelev by the arms and dragged him into the laboratory where he could breathe. They needed him.

They locked the door so no one else could enter through the office.

The lab scientists looked up. There were seven of them. Astonishment widened their eyes. They grabbed air rifles.

"Eight minutes!" Mike said. "Only eight minutes! Where the hell is Blenkochev?"

Carter swung his air rifle, knocking the closest scientist off his feet and back into a table. Glass vials and tubes smashed to the floor.

Through the only other doorway, his thick black hair a wild halo over his head, Blenkochev charged like a bull into the laboratory. He, too, locked the door.

His stout face was thick with anger. His impeccable clothing was disheveled. His hands were raw and bleeding.

"They've killed Larionov," the heavyset KGB leader said.

He grabbed a Silver Dove scientist, picked him up as if he were a rag doll, and threw him across the room at two other scientists who were frantically trying to decide who to shoot first. The three collapsed in a heap to the floor.

"Then I'll take care of the outside doors myself," Carter said.

But first the three had to secure the laboratory before the glass cage was opened or broken into and the lethal bacteria released.

Mike raised her air rifle as if it were an ax. A scientist dashed toward her on his way to attack Carter. As he passed, she smashed the rifle down onto his head. He stopped dead in his tracks, surprised. Then he crumpled to the floor.

Carter spun and kicked the sixth scientist in the nose. The

nose broke, the cartilage destroyed. The scientist yelled, grabbing his flattened nose as blood poured through his fingers.

Blenkochev picked up the last scientist by the front of his lab coat, swung him back and forth like a battering ram, then sent him skidding along a lab table as if he were a stein of beer. Microscopes flew off the table in a wake of metal and glass.

Carter stripped off his white snowsuit so that he was once again in his khaki clothes. He picked up Skobelev and shook him. Skobelev groaned.

"Wake up, dammit!" Carter said.

Blenkochev and Mike were already dragging the scientists into a corner where they could be better watched.

Someone pounded on the lab door. Carter looked with dismay at his watch. Mike stripped down to her khaki suit. Blenkochev still wore his blue one.

"Four minutes," Carter said grimly. "Skobelev!" He shook the Silver Dove leader again, then slapped his cheeks.

Skobelev's eyes opened. He frowned. Carter stood him on his feet.

"We're going," Carter told Blenkochev and Mike. "Keep the area secure. Don't let anyone in."

He reached for the door to the office.

"You're much too impertinent, N3," Blenkochev said.

He opened the door a crack and peered in, his air rifle ready. He nodded tersely and slipped into the office.

Behind Carter, Mike lifted her air rifle to guard the pile of semiconscious scientists.

Carter pushed Skobelev into the office. As he passed the desk, the Killmaster picked up Wilhelmina and slipped her in his pocket.

At the hall door, Blenkochev once again peered out. Voices, footsteps, and confusion echoed from the corridor.

"Very bad. Too many Doves," he told Carter. "Better let me handle it."

Before Carter could protest, Blenkochev stepped into the hall and closed the door.

The feet moved, slowed, stopped. There was a din of voices, so many that no individual one stood out. Then Blenkochev's voice predominated, the strong cultured Russian voice that commanded attention. Again the din rose up, overtaking Blenkochev.

Carter balanced Wilhelmina in his hand, ready.

Suddenly there was a shout, the voices unified. Curses filled the air. Feet pounded down the hall.

The door opened. Carter backed around it, Skobelev limp beside him. He raised his Luger.

"Hurry!" Blenkochev said, his big head coming around the door. "Everyone's gone. This way now. A short cut!"

He opened a door across the hall, then ran into a new corridor Carter had never been in.

"Only two minutes!" Carter said.

Dragging Skobelev, Carter ran behind Blenkochev past more offices and conference rooms.

"What did you tell them?" Carter asked.

"That you'd broken into the lab. Let out the bacteria. They believed it."

"Jesus Christ."

"In this building, it's best to keep religion out of it," the KGB czar observed.

Panting, he stopped in front of a heavy steel door. He took a breath.

"Inside are the controls for the electronic equipment in the installation," he said.

"Including the big outside doors?"

"Exactly."

Carter and Blenkochev stared at Skobelev.

"I've never liked you," Blenkochev said to Skobelev. "You're a sniveling little pansy. No guts. No heart. And worse yet, no brains."

Skobelev drew himself up and straightened his smudged

white silk three-piece suit.

"I don't have time to be tactful," Carter said, staring at Skobelev. "When we get in there, you lock those gates open. If you don't I'll kill you."

"If you kill me," Skobelev said arrogantly, "you'll never get the gates open. They close automatically when the alarm goes off. They're closed by now. Only a secret code will open them again."

Blenkochev picked Skobelev up by the back of the neck. He swung the smaller man like a pendulum.

"If you don't open them," Blenkochev said, "we're dead anyway. And *I'll* kill you. It's been a long time, but I remember how."

He dropped his air rifle to the floor and pulled a stiletto from a sheath inside his blue suit. He sliced down the front of Skobelev's jacket, through the silver dove on the heart. The jacket gaped open. Skobelev refused to look down, but a vein on his temple began to throb.

"I'd enjoy killing you," the KGB man said grimly. "A nice little traitor like you."

Carter looked at his watch.

"Thirty seconds."

He kicked open the door, air rifle ready.

Four dead, bloody bodies littered the floor. One of them was Lev Larionov, the former priest. The other three were Silver Dove technicians.

Carter looked at Blenkochev.

"Why I was late," Blenkochev said simply.

He shoved Skobelev into the room. The traitorous general stumbled, falling onto Larionov's corpse. He pulled himself up, his face pasty, wanting to recoil, but he refused to show any weakness. He smoothed his cut jacket and walked across the room to a computer console. For the moment, he was beaten.

Blenkochev followed while Carter watched one of the television screens that showed the giant front doors of steel.

They were closed as Skobelev had said. Inside the doors in the warehouse area, Silver Dove soldiers were handing out air rifles and ammunition.

Skobelev stood silently at the console. Blenkochev jammed a gun in his back. The Soviet general slowly reached a hand forward. Slowly the fingers pressed keys on the console. The monitor read, "Are you sure?" Impatient, Blenkochev pressed in "Yes." Colored lights flashed.

"Ten seconds," Carter said.

Slowly the doors began to open.

Firing, khaki-clad antiterrorist troops slipped in the widening crack.

"There're my men," Blenkochev said, his gaze fastened to the overhead monitors. "Yuri Somolov is leading. A good man. Reliable."

The Americans, New Zealanders, and British mixed with the Russians, firing at the white-clothed Silver Doves. Some darted toward the corners. Others knelt, holding their ground, refusing to retreat as the Doves mustered themselves in a furious attack. Bodies began to litter the floor. Still the invading force moved slowly but relentlessly on toward the back of the warehouse, toward the doors that led into the rest of the compound.

Skobelev turned, his face reset from fear to self-confidence, a still dangerous man. Even though his forces appeared to be losing, he had not given up. He was already figuring out how he was going to talk the Politburo out of his responsibility for the gone-wrong Silver Doves. Even before he was free of charges, he'd form another group. A fanatic was a person who redoubled his efforts once his aims were lost. Skobelev wasn't a supremacist as much as a man who blindly pursued a nonexistent goal no matter the cost to others.

Blenkochev gazed appraisingly at the wily general. The big KGB man knew, too, what was going to happen. His face said it was too much. He pulled back a massive fist and decked the traitorous general.

As Skobelev sprawled unconscious to the floor, Blenkochev looked around the room. Carter picked up a folding chair and set it behind him. Blenkochev nodded his thanks and sat. He tilted his head to watch the television screen. Crouching and firing, David Hawk and Chester ffolkes ran into the warehouse. They separated to improve their chances of making it.

The invading units fought onward. The Silver Doves made the international forces pay with injury and death for every inch they gained.

Blenkochev sighed and put his bloody hands on his legs. The hands trembled.

"I'm sorry about Anna," Carter said.

Blenkochev watched the battle on the screen.

"You loved her?" he said.

"Yes."

"At least she had that."

Blenkochev sat squat and solid on the chair, a sixty-eight-year-old agent who'd lost his daughter. He couldn't think about that. He'd wait to grieve until he was alone at home. Instead he watched with pleasure as the international units finally passed through the doors that led into the Silver Dove complex. Soon rifle fire echoed inside the miles of corridors.

Skobelev moaned and sat up.

"About the penicillin," Carter said. He looked at Blenkochev. "You diluted it?"

The K-GOL director was silent. He stared at the screens, tracking the battle. The hands seemed to tremble more.

"You diluted it, made money," Carter said. "Maybe you pocketed the profits yourself."

Skobelev's gaze moved from one agent to the other. He was beginning to understand.

"That's how you were able to buy off the newspaper in Düsseldorf," Carter said.

"What's past is past," Blenkochev said at last. He hadn't

wanted to say even that. "I paid for the newspaper myself."

Skobelev laughed and stood. He was shaky, but he held himself together as if he weren't. There was fresh determination about him.

"Not many alive today know that story!" General Skobelev said. "I'll have to remind Chernenko."

There was sudden pounding at the door. Carter went to it.

"N3!" It was Hawk's voice. "Open up!"

When Carter opened the door, Hawk and Colonel ffolkes were standing there, eyes bright with victory.

"It's secure, old man," ffolkes cheerfully told Carter. "It's a bloody mess out there, but the damned Doves won't be able to poison the world as they'd promised."

As ffolkes talked, Hawk brushed past Carter. He glanced at Blenkochev, his gaze level with appreciation for the Russian's cooperation. Then he strode directly to General Skobelev.

"Skobelev!" Hawk growled. "So you've found a new way to cause us trouble!"

Skobelev, suddenly unsure, backed toward Blenkochev. The mighty K-GOL man stood, glowering at the Silver Dove leader.

"I'll go back to Moscow," Skobelev said. "With Blenkochev."

"You think you'll get off scot-free?" ffolkes said, appalled.

Hawk watched the cagey Soviet general with interest.

"He has something to trade," Hawk decided.

"Penicillin," Blenkochev said curtly.

Hawk, ffolkes, and Carter looked at Blenkochev.

"I was following orders," Blenkochev said. No shame or remorse showed on his face as he used the ancient soldier's excuse to avoid responsibility. "Stalin's orders. We were making a better world. We all did things we wouldn't have done otherwise. It was after the war, and my country needed the money. Later, after Stalin died and Khrushchev de-

nounced him, the orders from higher up changed. If the
penicillin situation had occurred again, it would've been
because of individual decisions in the field, not orders from
the top.''

"So the old acts are now hidden," ffolkes said. "Against
policy.''

"Hidden as a substitute for forgotten," Hawk said.

"And when the past raises its ugly face, the Politburo runs
screaming," Carter said.

"I'm not proud of it," Blenkochev said, raising his head to
gaze around the room with his steely eyes. "I did what I had
to do. My duty. My country had to survive.''

"One wonders whether when the cost is so high the country deserves to survive," Carter said.

"It's not my job to decide that," Blenkochev said. "I only
do what's necessary.''

Skobelev laughed heartily. He hooked his thumbs inside
the waist of his pants and laughed at the joke.

"I'll remember that when I talk to Chernenko!" Skobelev
said.

Confidence had flooded back into the creator of the Silver
Doves. Skobelev had remembered what it was to be a Soviet
general. To be Chernenko's right hand. To be able to outwit
most of those who would succeed Chernenko. He knew once
again what it was to be so powerful that the lives of those
around him were in constant jeopardy to his whim.

Hawk and Blenkochev exchanged a long look. Each knew
that Skobelev accurately understood the situation. If Blenkochev's past came out, Blenkochev would have to be killed
or exiled, and—more important—Skobelev would have time
to build a new base of power from which he could destroy the
world.

Hawk had had enough of that. He raised his air rifle and
shot.

It was a good clean shot through Skobelev's heart. The
dead man stared surprised at Hawk. He put a hand up to

uselessly press against the gaping hole from which blood poured. Treachery was his, his stricken eyes seemed to say, and no one else had the intelligence for it.

Blenkochev watched thoughtfully, then nodded at Hawk. Hawk nodded soberly in return. They didn't like one another, but they understood their jobs.

In the Silver Dove valley, Carter stood outside the enormous double doors and smoked a cigarette. Around him, people shouted orders and engines roared into life.

The international antiterrorist troops were piling the defeated Doves into open trucks on the first leg of their return journey to Moscow and trial. The Doves were silent, their faces angry and fearful as they faced their new futures.

Into enclosed, heated trucks, the troops helped the women who'd been locked into the bowels of the mountain. They were women recruited around the world by Doves on their travels. Promised high wages and interesting work, they instead found themselves kidnapped and then deprived of all hope. Some held their heads high, proud to have triumphed by surviving. Others clutched one another, cowed by fears that would stain their futures.

Carter smoked his cigarette and walked along the mountain. His steps crunched on the hard snow.

Into a helicopter, protected in sealed lead containers, special mop-up troops loaded the vials of bacteria. They would go to a special laboratory in Geneva where the bacteria would be studied to learn its secrets and then, if there were no beneficial possibilities to it, it would be destroyed.

The Antarctic air was crisp and clear. Carter inhaled it in deep breaths and put out his cigarette. He strode down the valley, feeling his muscles strain. It made him know he was alive.

He rounded a bend in the valley to an area where it widened. He stopped and stared.

Ahead, standing in front of a helicopter, stood David

Hawk and Leon Blenkochev, the two powerful heads of
adversary secret agencies. They were completely alone. The
old enemies stood at arm's distance, talking in a field of
white. They were dressed in their snowsuits, Blenkochev's
stout figure in blue, and Hawk in khaki, a cigar jutting from
his mouth. The smoke blew into the air and quickly disappeared.

Carter smiled at the momentous, well-hidden occasion.

"Nick!"

Carter turned, and Mike ran to him.

"Here you are," she said. "I've been looking for you."

Carter nodded at Hawk and Blenkochev.

"The mountain has come to Mohammed," Carter said.
"But who's to say which of the two is the mountain?"

Astonished, Mike stared ahead.

The old foes maintained their distance. First one talked,
then the other. It was a polite conversation, dignified.

"What's it all about?" Mike wondered.

"I don't know," Carter said, "and I doubt that we'll ever
find out."

"Leslee Warner?" Mike said. "Anna Blenkochev? Pre-
cautions against future Silver Doves?"

"Maybe. Or maybe it's simply shop talk. The irritations of
running a secret agency."

"How hard it is to find good spies these days," Mike said
and smiled.

"The high cost of informers," he suggested. "Dealing
with superiors who don't appreciate the problems of being an
agency head."

Mike laughed quietly and slipped her arm through his.

"Come on," she said, pulling him back toward the activity in the valley. "They'll never tell us a thing."

"Where to?" Carter asked.

"I have a helicopter waiting for you, too," she said.
"Hawk's orders."

He looked at her suspiciously. She tugged on his beard.

"Vacation!" She laughed. "Trout! And no other women. You're very unreliable that way. No more falling in love! I'll give you your vacation," she promised, her eyes dancing, "the best damned vacation you've ever had!"

Carter laughed.

"I'll bet you will," he said.

DON'T MISS THE NEXT NEW
NICK CARTER SPY THRILLER

THE ASSASSIN CONVENTION

Carter recovered quickly from the stunning blow he had
received when the explosion slammed him against the wall of
rocks. He moved carefully past the smoldering, fiery wreck
that had once been a sleek warship and located the door of the
lighthouse. Light streamed out into the night, illuminating
the still-falling snowflakes. The impact of the explosion had
blown the door open. Carter followed the light, Wilhelmina
clasped in his hand.

He moved out of the light and leaned against the stone
wall, wanting to lob in two or three gas bombs but knowing
that he couldn't. If he could possibly save Steiner, he would.
He determined that the cruise missile was about to be fired,
he wouldn't hesitate, but he knew that it would take time for
the necessary codes to clear. And he hoped that the mysterious explosion that had destroyed the Polish warship had
slowed the plans of the people upstairs.

There was a little time, Carter thought; he would use it well.

Captain Nils Bridevell, proud of his boat and of his aim, headed the *Hanseatic Queen* northwest toward Copenhagen. The torpedo that his boat carried—and that many Danish fishing boats carried to ward off Russian trawlers and fishing boats that encroached on their territory—had done its job.

The captain had not received the full amount of money that had been promised him for this dangerous run, but he was leaving with the satisfaction of believing that he had killed the people who had double-crossed him and his crew.

The sight of that mighty destroyer going up like a Roman candle had been worth the trip.

Bridevell would never know the full ramifications of that explosion, but he was satisfied with the knowledge that he had totally disabled a Polish warship and, in all probability, had killed the trio that had so cheated him.

It would be a rough voyage back home, but a happy one. As for Lars Norrstrom, well, the big man had been in tight scrapes before and had escaped.

He would do it again.

Carter's patience paid off. One of the gunmen inside the lighthouse, concerned about the wind and snow that was streaming into the open door, decided to repair the damage.

Carter slipped his Luger into his pocket and snapped Hugo into his hand. He slipped up behind the guard, ran the stiletto across the man's throat, and watched the blood gush out and down the man's front. The man's weapon, propped against the staircase leading up through the lighthouse, was an AK-47.

The Killmaster waited until he was certain the guard was dead, then dragged him beneath the spiral staircase. He checked the Russian-made automatic rifle, found it ready to fire, and started slowly up the stone steps.

He found a second guard in the small circular room on the

next level. The man was peering through a tiny window at the burning destroyer. The sound of the storm outside had muffled Carter's footsteps. Carter moved like a shadow up behind the man and whacked him in the temple with the butt of the automatic rifle. Leaving nothing to chance, he cut the man's throat and left him to die on the stone floor.

It was different at the third level. Two guards lay on bunks in the cramped quarters. Carter waited in shadow and heard the beeping sounds of a computer keyboard from the level above. Time was of utmost importance now. The code was probably being punched in, proper responses were being fed back, and any minute now, the signal to fire a cruise missile from a NATO country would be given.

Once that happened, it didn't really matter if Carter succeeded in cleaning out the lighthouse. Time, at a premium to him now, would be meaningless—to the whole human race.

Carter made a bold decision. Although he preferred to work quietly and in secret until the last minute, he decided to let those at the level above know that they were not as safe as they thought. He raised the AK-47 and let fly with a rain of copper-sheathed bullets at the men lying on the bunks.

Both men were immediately awakened by the sound of Carter pulling back the firing mechanism. Both saw the rifle pointed their way and were reaching for their own weapons when the deadly rain came. The first man had half his head torn away. The second man felt a dull punching in his stomach. The noise of the AK-47 firing in that small enclosed space was ear-splitting.

The results were what the Killmaster expected. He heard shouts from above. He heard chairs scraping. He heard footsteps moving in panic.

He called out, "Steiner! Your wife and children are safe! I have a note from Helen! She, Peter, Jan, and Lisette are safe in Paris! If you haven't punched in all the code, stop now! You'll be exonerated because of circumstances."

The result that Carter hoped for came swiftly. Steiner, certain that the man below was telling the truth, surprised everyone around him by leaping from his chair at the computer terminal and fairly falling down the steep stone steps. Carter caught him before he slammed into the floor.

He quickly pulled the pins of two gas bombs, heaved them up the stairs, and yanked a stunned Neil Steiner after him as he headed down through the lighthouse.

Captain Lars Norrstrom and the *Little Mermaid* waited, engines purring smoothly.

"What the hell happened in there?" Norrstrom asked Carter. He'd heard the shots. "Are you ever going to tell me what this is all about?"

"Later!" Carter gasped. "Let's clear out for home!"

Once the boat moved away from the lighthouse, Carter explained a little of what had happened and of what they had prevented. Lars Norrstrom listened, fascinated.

"I know who sunk the destroyer," he said to Carter. "It had to be whatever captain they hired to take them there. Why he did it, I don't know. Well, if he can torpedo a destroyer, I can torpedo a lighthouse and make sure those people never cause trouble again."

With that, he maneuvered the boat south of the burning destroyer, and after lining up with a spot where the base of the lighthouse met the sea, he punched a button. Something long and slender leaped from near the bow of the boat, causing the *Little Mermaid* to shudder.

The torpedo ripped into stone and sent a column of flame up through the lighthouse at Point Lochsa.

"Now," Captain Lars Norrstrom said with a wide smile, "if your friends are still alive after that, you might as well give up. You are dealing with demons from hell and not human beings. I don't know who you are, mister, but I think your troubles from that bunch are over."

Carter watched the flames that glowed from the site of the lighthouse. The building, and everything and everyone in it, was now a charred pile of rubble.

Carter sighed with relief and exhaustion. Soon they would be back in Copenhagen. Then he would return to Paris to

Giselle, and Steiner would be reunited with his family. With the hypnotic throbbing of the twin diesel engines of the *Little Mermaid* in his ears and the image of the lovely Frenchwoman in his mind, Carter fell asleep where he sat. For the first time in almost two days, being out in the cold, the snow, and the driving wind didn't bother him a bit.

In his dream he was in a warm bed on Avenue St. Cloud, and he was enjoying every minute.

—From THE ASSASSIN CONVENTION
A New Nick Carter Spy Thriller
From Charter in September 1985

NICK CARTER

☐ 74965-8	**SAN JUAN INFERNO**		$2.50
☐ 14222-2	**DEATH HAND PLAY**		$2.50
☐ 45520-4	**THE KREMLIN KILL**		$2.50
☐ 52276-9	**THE MAYAN CONNECTION**		$2.50
☐ 06861-8	**THE BLUE ICE AFFAIR**		$2.50
☐ 51353-0	**THE MACAO MASSACRE**		$2.50
☐ 69180-3	**PURSUIT OF THE EAGLE**		$2.50
☐ 24089-5	**LAST FLIGHT TO MOSCOW**		$2.50
☐ 86129-6	**THE VENGEANCE GAME**		$2.50
☐ 58612-0	**THE NORMANDY CODE**		$2.50
☐ 88568-3	**ZERO-HOUR STRIKE FORCE**		$2.50

Prices may be slightly higher in Canada.

Available at your local bookstore or return this form to:

C CHARTER BOOKS
Book Mailing Service
P.O. Box 690, Rockville Centre, NY 11571

Please send me the titles checked above. I enclose _____ Include 75¢ for postage
and handling if one book is ordered; 25¢ per book for two or more not to exceed
$1.75. California, Illinois, New York and Tennessee residents please add sales tax.

NAME _____

ADDRESS _____

CITY _____ STATE/ZIP _____

(allow six weeks for delivery.)   A8